WRITTEN WORKS OF GLEN CHESNUT

Glen Chesnut

ISBN: 978-1-7330159-2-9
LCCN: 2020909580

Front cover design by Valerie Turpen.
Edited by Janice Lalley.
Book design and layout by Donna Tate.

Printed in the United States of America.
First printing edition 2020.

www.ellensarkisianchesnut.com

Dedicated to Glen Chesnut
WRITER AND ARTIST,
who never wavered in his commitment
to living a creative life.

b. Amarillo, Texas: March 4, 1930
d. Alameda, California: July 6, 2017

Glen Chesnut

WRITTEN WORKS
OF GLEN CHESNUT

FORWARD

I walked into a near-square room: neat, bordered on all four sides with low bookshelves topped with magazine racks of *Nerve Cowboy* and *Over the Transom* (small print publications). Interspersed throughout the room were photographs, 3-D artwork, and photographs of Glen Chesnut. His artwork and canvases (some framed) hung on all walls creating a cozily, art-populated space that seemed to quietly invite creative endeavors.

I was immediately struck by the impact of realizing all this artwork was created by Glen, not collected pieces someone might decorate his office workspace with! Little did I know when I agreed to work with his widow Ellen Chesnut to organize his poetry and prose that I was dealing with a prodigious artist with multidisciplinary skills.

In one corner of Glen's office, under the shadow of a bookcase and window, a tidy stack of banker's boxes contained "most" of Glen's written works. Ellen, who had lost Glen the previous year, had diligently collected the materials while recovering from the grieving process. I would ultimately read, and with Ellen's input, select works to go into this book of "poetry and prose."

Little did we know that it would take us more than a year to go through all of Glen's written works. This included handwritten, typewritten, and computer-printed works, sometimes in duplicate or multiple versions.

Hidden by the back of a chair, we found Glen's personal computer, the self-effacing, small Macbook Pro (obviously a very important laptop since it was given a whole desktop to itself!).

The room also ended up having files in various folders, versions, and formats needing, at times, special software to open the files. This was plainly a complex task (even if initially unforeseen) of organizing, sorting, and curating a lifetime of work by Glen Chesnut. What a pleasant job it became due to the convivial nature of Ellen and me approaching the task as treasure hunters out to discover all this man had conjectured and produced. We did not leave a floppy disk or manilla folder unopened. What we found was astounding, even to Ellen, who knew the tremendous work ethic of Glen–her partner of many decades.

When we finished cataloging Glen's lifetime of written works, we found he had produced: 48 short stories, 67 prose-poems, 688 poems (of all types, haiku to free-form), and one play.

We also unearthed some of the "words with images" he produced as well as his experiments (as seen in his handwritten notes and on his computer files). Glen would morph material across genres between a short story, flash fiction, prose-poetry, and pure poetry. In essence, this was the extent of Glen's boundless creativity, which was not to be bothered by boundaries.

With the above in mind, a plan developed between Ellen and me to select pieces for an anthology of his written works: We agreed it would include "the best of the best." This would mean we would read EVERY single completed piece he had written and vote on its merits to be included in this book.

So this organic process of discovering new pieces, re-classifying genres, reading, editing, and accessing "bestness" took the best part of a year. And although it was arduous, it was an amicable process. During the reviews, we discovered Glen's indubitable sense of humor and quiet insights into life's inanities or mysteries. But since we couldn't include all his works, we advocated for certain pieces to make the cut since so many of Glen's works, especially his poems, were heartbreakingly good.

In the end, we decided to organize this anthology into three main sections: flash fiction, poetry, and short stories. The poetry section was further divided into five broad and rangy themes.

It may also be of interest for you to know that GEC produced and left behind countless works of visual arts in the form of "words with images," sculptures, drawings, and sketches.

So yes. There will be a second book of Glen's amazing artwork.

But for now, enjoy!

—RAMYA SRINIVASAN

Content

PART II
Poetry

Sea Poems

Love In Many Ways

Memories and Musings: Personal

On Time and Aging

Mysteries, Oddities, and Ironies - Philosophic Reflections

PART III
Short Stories

GLEN CHESNUT:
Raconteur, Painter, Photographer, Horse Lover

If the impossible were possible, I would channel Glen Chesnut. I imagine his immediate response to an introduction to his work would go something like this: "No work worth its salt needs an introduction. Just read it." Knowing Glen, he would use more colorful language. Open the pages of this volume. Read Glen's poetry and prose, feast on his images. Meanwhile, brooking Glen's ire, I continue.

In his work and art, Glen is alive. Glen chronicled his experiences. He was a raconteur and in this volume, *WRITTEN WORKS OF Glen Chesnut*, he continues being that keen-eyed storyteller. His writing is honest, accessible, unvarnished. But don't be duped, there's a well-honed, well-voiced experience in these pieces. A bit of grit and wry, too.

Like his work, you knew where you stood with Glen. He expressed candor and empathy for his "subjects." Well, most of them. There is that "suit" on the cell phone in "Overheard in a Public Restroom." As the poem says, "This guy never missed a beat." Nor does our poet. Good for us, Glen is a skilled eavesdropper.

Where did this original being come from? Glen Chesnut grew up in the 30s in Amarillo, Texas. A son of parents who worked cattle ranges; the family moved a lot. From his early childhood, Glen gained a love of horses. Glen was a cowboy for decades before returning to school and eventually earning a B.A. from Fresno State in 1954. After graduation, Glen was drafted into the army, shipped to Germany. The army, not his heart song but fueled a love of travel.

After wanderlust set in, Glen became licensed with the Marine Firemen's Union as a merchant seaman in 1957. He spent 23 years, half of his time at sea, the other half on land. During this time, Glen docked in North Beach, the bohemian section of San Francisco. Glen wrote poems and prose. In the mid-sixties, Glen shifted his focus to painting, self-taught. During this time, Glen met painter, high school teacher, and historian, Ellen Sarkisian. They married in 1972. Later, Glen would return to writing. In 2006, Glen and Ellen moved to Alameda, CA, where Glen became affiliated with the Frank Bette Center for the Arts.

I first encountered Glen at the weekly reading series at Keane's 3300 Club. The 3300 Club was an institution as a working-class bar and vibrant poetry and spoken word scene. Located in the Mission District of San Francisco, it was hosted by its owner Nancy Keane, herself a painter and poet. Sadly, the 3300 Club was destroyed by fire in June 2016. Nancy Keane has passed. The band of rogue poets and troubadours dispersed.

It was the poetry press Nancy Keane founded, which published Glen's first collection of poems, Taking the Bull by the Horns in 1966. Glen was a frequent feature at the 3300 Club and always performed on the open mic. Glen approached the mic, standing tall with his signature mustache, no artifice to this man. I recall Glen saying on more than one occasion, "There's no damn 't' in my last name; I'm the nut without the 't.'"

Well read, well-traveled, and published, Glen's second collection was Of Time and the Leaky Faucet. His poems and prose have appeared widely, including in *Zyzzyva*, *Staplegun*, *Word-Wrights*, *33 Review*, *Main Street Rag*, and *Over the Transom*.

Speaking of *Over the Transom*, many of Glen's photographs are captured on the covers of this literary magazine, edited by Jonathan Hayes. His prose and poetry are richly included. I'm particularly drawn to Glen's sketch in *Over the Transom*, issue 21 with its handwritten title like a found poem: "Sketch on a napkin of a man walking down Broadway. Seen through the window of Mike's Pool Hall, North Beach, 2 a.m. 1967."

Over the Transom, issue 29 celebrates the life and art of Glen Chesnut. A fitting tribute. Worthy the read.

Let's spotlight a few of the writings in this collection.

"A Bag of Tricks" is a surreal dream poem. Like all dreams, it is full of twists, turns, and wisdom. Just listen: "You can not hide in the home of childhood," he says. "Nor is there a best place to take a chance. No use following that thread into the past or searching for a vivid encounter on a dark city street. ...It's all no more than silence in a cloud of smoke."

Another poem, "I Should Write a Poem," opens with the line, "Today is such a beautiful spring day, I should write a poem." This piece proceeds with a list of "I shoulds" ending in an image that upends it all. So like Glen; you can see him grinning, with a kind "gotcha."

Glen's love of horses shows up repeatedly in his work. Take a look at his poem "Horsepower" in this collection. Irritated by spiny, speeding cars, the poem leaps to an appreciation of a team of horses digging in to do the task. I'm also reminded of Glen's stunning black and white photo of a horse in Over the Transom #21 back cover, 1956, Amsterdam.

A life doesn't evaporate; it's an invitation to linger, to remember, to celebrate. So I imagine this interview:

Interviewer: So Glen, tell us about your work, your life, your favorite writers, go-to musicians, your writing practice. What advice do you have for younger writers? What's your favorite bar? What books are on your bookshelves? What are your favorite stories?

What do you like to cook if you cook? What is the name of your first horse? You are organizing a literary dinner, who do you invite? Tell us everything.

Glen: Thanks. I'll be brief. To quote myself from "Two Trees Making Love," I think I'll go home and see what mood Ellen's in.

We are lucky because Glen wrote, performed, and published his poetry, prose, flash fiction. He was a photographer, a painter. He was a mentor. Glen is one of those two trees.

Kit Kennedy

Walnut Creek, CA

Kit is a poet, photographer, and also blogs about poetry and small dishes (*http://poetrybites.blogspot.com*).

She is a Poet-In-Residence with the SF Bay Times, and Poet-In-Residence with Ebenezer Lutheran "herchurch," located in San Francisco.

PART I
Flash Fiction

D. Chesnut

THE ARTIST'S LAMENT
Over the Transom

You know that old cliché: She walked out on me. Well, she walked out on me.

She said, "It's me or the booze."

I look at my sad reflection in the mirror across the bar. I take a sketchpad from my pocket and begin to draw my image—slashing lines with my ballpoint pen. I draw until the man in the sketch is barely visible behind the lines. I take a long look at the drawing.

Then I wave to the bartender and say, "Bring me one more of the same."

A BAG OF TRICKS

I awaken to the barking of the dog. Then abruptly, the barking stops, replaced by whimpers of obedience. Someone is knocking at my door. I hesitate. Who can it be at this late hour?

The knocking continues. I open the door. He has a youthful face framed by long gray hair. He carries a backpack and on his face a smile. The dog is gnawing on a meaty bone.

"What is it? What is it that you want?"

"I'm here to show you my bag of tricks."

And, like pulling an arrow from a quiver, he pulls a paper bag from his backpack. He blows into the paper bag, inflating it like a paper balloon.

"Please don't bother me with your bag of tricks."

I close the door, and as I do, I hear the pop of an exploding paper bag. Suddenly, I'm surrounded by the red, stained walls of a large, cold room. Water drips from the ceiling into rusty metal buckets—plink, plink, plink... The walls of the room seem to be moving. But when I look closer, I can see it is only crawling red camellias.

A blindfolded man in a hospital gown is gathering up the scattered pages of a manuscript. When he bends over, his backside is exposed. I pick up one of the pages and read: "Things that only bedlam can teach you, and the memory of impermanent things." I drop the page and watch it flutter to the floor.

I cross the room to a small, barred window. Hanging from a tree is the limp remains of a large bird of prey. In a meadow, a group of happy peasants on a picnic. They are playing cards and wagering which one will be the angel.

A man in a white coat enters the room. "You can not hide in the home of childhood," he says. "Nor is there a best place to take a chance. No use following that thread into the past or searching for a vivid encounter on a dark city street."

And over his shoulder, as he leaves the room, he says, "It's all no more than silence in a cloud of smoke."

A bed in the corner of the room, covered with my mother's patchwork quilt, reminds me that I'm tired and sleepy. I lie down and immediately fall asleep.

When I awake, light is streaming through my bedroom window. I lie there thinking, trying to extricate myself from my dream. I hear the dog scratching at the door. I open the door. The dog looks up at me. He has a bone in his mouth, and at his feet is a crumpled paper bag.

AT THE LIBRARY CAFE

After checking out my book, I go to the library cafe, order a large coffee, find myself a table, and sit and sip my coffee and thumb through my book. Then I hear this one-way conversation over to my right. I turn and look, and this little old lady wearing a fake leopard-skin coat and a red stocking cap pulled down around her ears is talking to an empty chair. Pretending to read my book, I listen in.

"What did she know? Nothing, that's what. She wouldn't listen to me. It was Doug: Doug this and Doug that. It was Doug alright—Doug digging his own grave. God, this coffee is awful! I told her, leave that man before he takes you with him. Two of a kind, the both of them. When summer comes, I'm going to the beach. Warm sand on my cold feet. Cold and fog... Florida would be nice, but I can't stand mildew. I should've told her what that man tried to do. Doug...God, Morris would've killed him. The Morris code. Thank you, Morris, for your social security. I like cats, and Morris liked dogs, but we never let that come between us.

"Doug liked anything that moved. I tried to tell her, but she wouldn't listen. And she still puts flowers on his grave, after what he did to her. Let's see, do I have milk at home? I should've made a list. Write it down. I even told her in writing. Now she's mad at me, and all I did was tell her the truth. The truth shall make you free. The truth cost me a friend. But I don't need her. I got too many friends as it is. Anyway, I got to go get some milk for my kitty cat."

She gets up abruptly and walks out with quick little steps, carrying a shopping bag. And I return to my book. The title of which is *Skull Juices* by Douglas Blazek.

OVERHEARD IN A PUBLIC RESTROOM

I was taking a piss the other day in a public restroom, and I heard this man in one of the stalls talking loudly. From the way he was talking, I assumed he was talking to himself. He sounded like one of those crazed people I see occasionally rambling down the street, delivering an angry diatribe against the world and any and everyone in it.

"Who does that son of a bitch think he is? Yeah, that's right, I'm on to him. He thinks he's got me by the balls. Hey, when it comes to squeezin' balls, he ain't seen nothin' yet.

"Oh, don't worry, I'm cool, I'm cool, I'll pick my time. But that turd is going to answer to me, for I am one hell of a turd-wacker. Yes, you have my permission to quote me on that. That bastard puts out a worse stink than the shit comin' out of my bowels right now. Yes, I'm taking a shit. And I'd like to eat that fucker and shit him out and flush him down like that." And I heard the toilet flush. "You hear that? That's what I'm going to do. I'm going to flush that piece of shit. Oh, man, I'm startin' to feel good all over just thinkin' about it. They ain't nothin' like gettin' even with a prick, a dirty rotten prick."

By this time, I was washing my hands. I heard the stall door open, and in the mirror above the washbasin, I saw this guy dressed in a dark suit walk by talking on a cell phone. As he walked by, I heard him say, "I'm on my way. Meet me there."

During that whole monologue, it never occurred to me that he was talking on a cell phone. This guy never missed a beat. How did he wipe his ass, pull up his pants, and put his shirttail in and, at the same time, keep talking on his cell phone? This guy was smooth. I'm glad I'm not the person he was out to get. And he looked tough, too. Hell, he didn't even wash his hands after taking a shit.

CHINCHES

I wanted to immerse myself in the Spanish language. So, I went to Guadalajara, Mexico. I chose Guadalajara because I like the way the word rolls off the tongue, especially when a Mexican says it.

I rented an apartment—sixty-five dollars a month, fully furnished, all ready for housekeeping. I went to a nearby market, bought bread, eggs, ham, can goods, and beer. Ah yes, beer. I made two trips for the beer.

I got all settled in, cooked myself some eggs, laid back on my comfy couch, and took a nap. When I woke up, it was dark, and I could hear the sounds of mariachi music coming from the Cantina Bonita on the corner across the street. I splashed cold water on my face and headed for the Cantina—to soak up some local color, I told myself.

She was the only one sitting at the bar, so I sat next to her, one stool between us. She had trashy good-looks, and her name was Lucha. We talked. I bought her drinks. She made it clear that she made her living off the gringos in the neighborhood. When I suggested that we move our little party to my apartment, Lucha was ready.

We crossed the street, had one more drink, then headed for the bed. We made love, and Lucha was good; she enjoyed her work. We took a shower and went at it again. Then we rolled over and fell asleep.

How long we slept, I do not know, but we both woke up at the same time. I felt as if I was lying on a bed of living nails. We jumped out of bed. I flicked on the light. The white sheet was crawling with tiny red bugs. Then, as soon as the light hit them, like magic, they disappeared, leaving our bloodstains on the sheet.

"Chinches! Chinches!" Lucha cried, "Dios mio, chinches!" Lucha's back was covered with red marks, and my back felt as if it was on fire.

I cleaned Lucha's back the best I could. She got dressed. And out of guilt, I gave her twice her usual fee. Then, she was gone.

As I stood naked in my apartment, the thought occurred to me: at least those chinches waited until we were through making love before they made their move.

I also added a new word to my Spanish vocabulary. I learned the Spanish word for bedbug—the hard way.

And I continued standing there naked listening to the mariachi music still playing at the Cantina Bonita.

GIANT FLIES

The flies that come into my house seem to come one at a time, always a huge, fat, lumbering thing whose ability to stay airborne defies the laws of physics.

I watch it slowly fly around the room, droning like one of those World War II bombers. Then, inevitably, it heads for the window and lands on one of the slats of the Venetian blinds, with great relief, I'm sure. It perches there for a while, catching its breath, I suppose. Then, wishing to return to the great outdoors, it attacks the window.

I never bother to kill one of these monster flies. I take an almost sadistic pleasure in watching it beat its head against the windowpane. At the same time, I feel sorry for it, but not sorry enough to open the window or to put it out of its misery with one quick swat of a rolled-up newspaper.

It buzzes and buzzes and butts its head against the windowpane, rests a while on a Venetian slat, then goes at the window again—over and over until the end.

I get tired of watching. I go about my business. Later, I remove the dead fly from the window sill.

But I can't help wondering why these giant flies are always alone. And they seem so lonely, too. Are they pariahs, flies so huge they couldn't fit in? Perhaps the normal flies banded together and said, "You're not welcome. You're a freak. You eat too much, and our women are afraid to have sex with you. Best you take a hike."

So they become lonely rogues—always moving on, probably looking for a little companionship. Somehow they find their way into my house, slowly buzz around the room, find nothing of interest here; then decide to leave, and they head for the light shining through the window. And there they die a slow, horrible death from exhaustion, trying to solve the mystery of that transparent wall.

KELSO'S CAFÉ

It was summertime in a small town. It was warm, and it was Saturday night. The bars had just closed, and Millard and I were in Kelso's Café, drinking coffee and waiting for our burgers. We were laughing and having fun; that's all we were doing.

Mrs. Kelso, who was screwing the cook behind her husband's back, and everybody but her husband knew it, came over to our booth and told us we'd have to go, that we were creating a disturbance. Truth was, she thought we were laughing at her and that thing she had going with the cook.

We didn't leave, Millard and I. We just sat there laughing and having fun. We didn't care if we got our burgers or not. What we didn't know was that Mrs. Kelso had called the cops. Here he was, standing at our table: white Stetson, khaki uniform, cowboy boots, and a .38 special hanging low on his thigh, like a western-movie gunfighter.

He looked at Millard, who was about 6'5". Then he looked at me and said, "Get out!"

I said, "What for?" And that's as far as I got.

He grabbed my head with his two big hands, like you would a cantaloupe, and dragged me out the café door. Out on the sidewalk, he let me go.

A crowd was forming, and I was saying, "Why did you do that? Why did you do that?

You almost broke my neck!"

The cop was crouched down low, a crazy smile on his face, rubbing his fist in the palm of his hand. He wanted to hit me, but the crowd was on my side.

Then I saw the other cop sitting in his car across the street. I walked over to make a complaint.

"That partner of yours is crazy," I said.

"I know that," he said. "But there ain't nothin' I can do about it."

I had a sore neck for a month after that. But not long after my neck healed up, Mr. Kelso came home early and caught the cowboy cop in bed with Mrs. Kelso. The cop's .38 special was hanging on a chair, so Mr. Kelso, who knew how to use guns, slipped it out of the holster and shot the cowboy cop right between his startled eyes.

Mr. Kelso served a short stretch for manslaughter. Mrs. Kelso got a divorce and married the cook, who was a lot more forgiving than Mr. Kelso.

LETTER FROM HENRY

His letter was somewhat frightening, but knowing him, it was not surprising. And I knew there was nothing I could do for him—he made that clear. All I could do was watch and wait to see how it all played out.

Dear Glen,

After many sizzling afterthoughts, I am now facing the brown unknown. No more white thighs or moist beginnings—that easy glide to slick penetration. No more the pleasure of delinquent entry. I see a luminous fog spanning the ditch. It's a cold, frightening vision—a chilling visitor. I've been holed up here for months now, waiting for a confrontation with the law. And, hell, no one comes! What is it with those bastards? Do they expect me to give myself up?

I may be crazy, but I'm no fool. And I don't need anybody's ridged approval. And I don't need anybody's verbal filigree—the cutting edge, the cutting hedge, the splitting wedge. But I do want my words to fit together like the stones in an Inca wall. That's important. All the rest is jazzed-up fortune cookie bullshit. Jesus! I feel like I'm surrounded by all the 12 animals of the Chinese zodiac, and all my days are nothing but x marks on the calendar! I just can't seem to make a move.

I can identify with the quivering of an atom at absolute zero. And it will take more than a freeze-dried smile to thaw me out. What's going to happen? Who knows? And I'm not sure I want to know. Wanting to know the future is like wanting tomorrow to arrive before today. But I do know this: the history of the world is written on my wallpaper; maybe the future, too, if I could only read it. Right now, all I see is the conductor waving from the last car as the train leaves the station. That's the train I should have caught.

But things could be worse. There could be a bunch of hellish guests moving about my four rooms. And let me add this before the creatures of the deep start landing on my table: if the timber wolf can make a comeback, maybe there's still hope for me. And although we keep trying, we haven't taken the twinkle out of the stars... yet. Anyway, Glen, there's nothing you can do. I'm all alone in this. Will the unthinkable become the inevitable?... I wait.

Your friend,

Henry

THE COUPLE

I watch them come into the library café. He's wearing a dark blue suit, a light blue shirt, and a maroon tie. She's wearing a tan suit and an off-white blouse.

They mosey up to the counter. She follows three paces behind him. Their arms are folded across their bodies. He gets a coffee and a bagel. She gets nothing.

They sit in a booth facing each other. He sips his coffee, pinches off small bits from his bagel. She sits with her head down, arms still folded across her body, a forlorn expression on her face. I watch them.

He sips his coffee, crumbles his bagel, and looks at her across the table. Then he looks around as though gathering himself together. He slides his cup to her side of the table, then slowly gets up and moves over next to her.

With his elbow on the table, he rests his cheek against his fist, his head turned toward her. He begins to talk to her. She begins to cry. She puts her hands over her face. He continues to talk. Her shoulders heave. He pinches off a small piece of bagel, eats it chewing slowly. Her shoulders cease to heave. He swallows his bagel and begins to talk.

She takes her hands from her face and dries her eyes with a napkin. She looks at him and speaks.

An expression close to a smile appears on her face. They look at each other. Her eyes are open wide—a look of expectation. Still, they do not touch. He leans back and folds his arms. She looks down at the table. And there they sit, each in his/her own world.

I finish my coffee and go for seconds. Still they sit. Finally, the woman looks at him. He leans his head against his hand. She begins to talk and slowly shake her head from side to side.

She's animated. He runs his fingers through his thick hair. She continues to talk. She's pressing him. She's gained the initiative. He seems to sink into himself. She reaches over and breaks off a piece of his bagel. She chews the bagel and looks at him, slumped over like a beaten man. She breaks off more bagel and continues to talk. She touches his shoulder—the first time they have touched.

He comes to life and puts his arm around her. She leans her head on his chest. I see a smile on her face. His face is devoid of emotion.

They get up from the booth, adjust their clothing, and then walk out of the coffee shop holding hands. She has a spring in her step. He looks confused. I continue working on my second cup of coffee.

THE HIGH SCHOOL ENGLISH CLASS

"Class, next week," the teacher said, "we have two marvelous poets coming to read to you their poetry." But the teacher didn't tell the class that she met one of these marvelous poets in a gritty, blue-collar bar on Mission Street called the 3300 Club. He'd had a few beers, and he promised to scare up another marvelous poet for this marvelous poetry reading.

All week the teacher put the class in a poetry mode. They read, wrote, and talked about poetry. On the day of the reading, marvel of marvels, the two marvelous poets didn't show up. The teacher was disappointed. No, better to say, she was pissed. But to salvage what she could, she had the class write what they had learned from the experience. Here is a condensed sampling of what she got:

I'll never marry a poet.
What I learned this week was a waste of time.
Poetry sucks.
Poets don't make much money, do they?
I like poetry, but I don't like poets.
If I told you what I really learned, I'd have to use dirty words.
Poets have a hard time saying what they mean.
Poets don't keep their word.
At least poets don't harm the environment.
Maybe those two poets got lost.
I don't care. I still want to meet a real live poet.
I didn't learn much of anything, and I hope we won't be tested on this.
I learned that poetry is pretty useless and maybe poets too.
The only poetry I like is Rap. Can we get a rapper to come to class?
Those poets didn't show, but hey, that's cool.

After a quick perusal of the students' papers, the teacher announced, "Next week, students, we will take up the short story."

THE SPIDER STRATEGY

I open my windows to the flies, let them enter my four dark rooms to feed my spiders. I never kill a spider. I let them range freely through my rooms, spin their lovely webs as they will. Sometimes when I look in the mirror just right, I think I look like a spider, but I can't spin a web, so I know I'm not one. Anyway, I don't dwell on it.

If I did, I'd go crazy, for from time to time, I think I look like a lot of things. Just this morning, I swear I looked just like a ball-peen hammer. That scared me a little. The thought came to me: god, I could be picked up and used as a weapon!—maybe to squash a spider, even! I feel a lot better when I look like Madame Butterfly or Charles Atlas. My best friend, whom I met only a couple of weeks ago, dropped by the other day, and he looked around and said, good lord, you're letting the spiders take over this place. I tried to explain to him the ecological wisdom behind it all, but I don't think he bought it. He looked very uneasy, and he didn't stay long, so I guess that's another best friend I'll never see again.

I think I'll give up on best friends and stick to casual acquaintances. Too bad I can't spin some sort of web to catch friends, like the spiders do to catch flies, only an invisible web where the victims aren't aware that they've been caught, but they are, as surely as in a steel trap. Now that I think about it, there is such a web. It's called charm or charisma. I see a lot of things when I look in the mirror, but I never see charm or charisma. So much for my invisible web.

Anyway, I read where el niño will bring us a large fly population; at least, my spiders will be happy. I also read where, in the end, dark matter will light the void, which won't make anybody happy.

PART II
Poetry

Sea Poems

WAITING FOR SEAMAN'S PAPERS

San Francisco, Greyhound Bus Depot, 1957.
Hired on as clerk in novelty concession
in center of terminal waiting room.
Terminal waiting room—
sounds ominous doesn't it? It was.
Sold everything from bubble gum
to handguns. I lasted 3
surrealistic days before I was terminated.

1st day: Learning the ropes. 8 hours
watching all those searching people
coming and going, listening to the
announcements of arrivals and departures.
I burn up a man's driver license
in the laminating machine—
a poor man in bib overalls, headed
for god-knows-where, walks off
with a hand full of ashes, mumbling to himself.
I still feel bad about that one.
2nd day: Seems like same people coming and going.
Same announcements of arrivals and departures.
A customer asks to see a handgun.
I take the pistol from the case
and hand it to him. He points
the pistol at me and says,
"Hand over all your cash
and make it snappy!
I've got a bus to catch!"
I reach over the counter
and take back the pistol.

The customer laughs and says,
"Just practicing," and walks away.

3rd day: More of same people coming and going.
More of same announcements of arrivals and departures.
But surprise: Toward end of shift, old flame
from hometown comes through terminal.
She sees me. We have big reunion at concession stand.
I ask boss if I can leave early.
He eagerly agrees.

4th day: The boss has my check ready
when I arrive.

One week later, seaman's papers come through.
Week after that, I'm on a ship
bound for the South Pacific.

A NIGHT IN LA UNION

I opened my eyes
and all I saw was darkness.
It was silent and all I heard
was the ringing in my ears.
Then the thought exploded
in my head: Where in the hell am I?
The question pulled me
to a sitting position.
My feet hit the floor.
My head was too heavy for my neck.
My chin lolled against my chest.

Then it hit me: I was in a
whore's cubical
behind the Texas Bar
in La Union, El Salvador.
What time was it? I knew it was late;
the jukeboxes were silent.
I groaned, "Oh, Christ!
I've missed the ship!"

My watch was gone.
I couldn't find my underwear.
To hell with underwear.
I found my pants, my shirt
and shoes, but no socks.
Who would want my
underwear and socks?
My money was gone—
no surprise there,
but they left me my wallet.

Somehow I made it to the street.
No life anywhere. But I'm in luck;
the one and only La Union taxi
is parked on the street
with the driver asleep behind the wheel.
I wake him up. He's happy to get
this unexpected fare.
We rattle off toward the dock.
I didn't tell him I had no money.

When we reached the gate at the top of the hill
overlooking the pier, I saw all the lights.
The ship was still there.
Boy, I thought, How lucky can you be?
I told the driver I had no money
but I'd go get some.
He said, "Give me your shirt."
Which I did,
then ran for the ship.

In my little steel fo'c'sle
all humming and vibrating
from the ship's machinery
I crawled into my bunk and smiled
thinking of how much fun
I must have had.

SAILING TO THE CANARIES

We left Casablanca
on the *SS Mariposa*
(It means butterfly in Spanish)
headed for the Canary Islands.
Sailing along the coast of Africa,
a strong offshore wind came up
blowing from the east, off the Sahara.
We could see it coming—
a great orange cloud.
And then it was upon us,
and the ocean disappeared.
We were sailing through a sandstorm.
The sandblasted-ship rolled and pitched.
All ventilators were shut down.
It was difficult to breathe the hot, stifling air.
And just when we all thought
we would suffocate,
the sandstorm was over, the sea was calm
and the sun was shining.
The sailors were on deck with hoses
washing down the ship,
and both the Mariposa and the day were sparkling
as we docked in the port of Santa Cruz
on the island of Tenerife.

I saw no canaries
in the Canary Islands.
But a lovely lady of the waterfront
had a parrot that spoke Spanish.
The parrot said, "Como esta, como esta?"
And I said, "Muy bien."

And the parrot said, "Muy bien, muy bien."
And the lady said, "Muy bien."
And it was. Everything was muy bien
that afternoon in Santa Cruz
on the island of Tenerife.

THE COLONEL

Guadalajara
high, dry, and windy.
After the bullfight
I have an early evening cerveza
in a nearby whorehouse.
The sun is going down, and
the fading orange light
filters through the shutters.
3 young whores sit at a table playing cards.
The whorehouse madam sits behind the bar.
Mariachis sing from the jukebox.
A man in uniform steps into the doorway.
He stands silhouetted in the sundown light.
He looks about the room,
then walks straight to my table.
Khaki uniform, gold braid on his cap,
ribbon salad on his chest,
a pistol hanging on his hip, and
an unfriendly smile full of teeth on his face.
He pulls out a chair and joins me uninvited.
"De dónde es usted?"
Where are you from?
"Soy de Los Estados Unidos."
I am from the United States.
"Soy de los Estados Unidos también—
los Estados Unidos de Mexico."
I am from the United States also—
the United States of Mexico.
He asks me what I do. I tell him I'm a seaman.
He tells me I'm a long way from the ocean.
Then he points to the insignia on his shoulder

and says he's a colonel in the army.
The madam comes over to our table,
and the colonel orders tequila.
Then he says, "You drink with me."
"OK," I say. "I'll have another Corona."
"No," he says. "You have tequila."
"No," I say. "I don't want tequila."
"Yes," he says. "You will drink tequila."
The madam hurries to the bar
and brings us 2 tequilas, lemon and salt.
The 3 whores have stopped playing cards.
The mariachis still sing from the jukebox.
The colonel throws back his tequila,
sighs, and sucks on a lemon.
"Drink!" he says. And I sip on my cerveza.

"No, you do not understand. Drink the tequila!"
I shake my head, and the colonel pulls his pistol.
He smiles and points the pistol between my eyes,
and says, "Now you will drink the tequila."
And I do. I drink the tequila.
It's the only smart thing to do.
The colonel lays the pistol on the table
and orders 2 more tequilas.
The madam is showing signs of fear,
and the whores are definitely alert.
The colonel raises his tequila
and waits for me to pick up mine.
"Salud," he says. He taps my glass,
and together we knock back our tequilas.
The colonel sucks on a lemon,
and I take a pull on my cerveza.
The colonel is all smiles. He's feeling good.

He gets up from the table and pulls
one of the whores to the dance floor.
He leaves the pistol on the table.
It's a beautiful shiny thing—
chrome-plated with mother-of-pearl handle.
He knows I will not touch it.
The colonel has the cheeks of the whore's ass
cupped in both his hands. Over the whore's shoulder,
he smiles at me as they sway on the dance floor.
This is my chance. I get up and rush out the door.
Over the music, I can hear the colonel laugh.
And I distinctly hear him say,
"El gringo no tiene huevos!"
The gringo has no balls!

It's dark now, and I walk down the dusty street
debating if I should chance
another whorehouse.

LOADING COFFEE IN SAN JOSE DE GUATEMALA

The sea, deep blue on the horizon,
comes in green around the anchored ship
and rolls on rising land swells shoreward,
where bottom-drag and undertow
pull the deeper water back
and bend the lunging foam crests down
to white froth lathering
the black sand beach of San Jose.

The ship, straining at the hook,
heaves on the mounting land swells,
as grinding winches hoist
the sacks of coffee up from barges,
swinging them abeam and down
where knotty-muscled stevedores—
barefoot, brown, and naked to the waist—
hump the heavy sacks in the oven heat of the holds.

Aft, on the canopied fantail, a seaman
lying on a bed of coiled mooring lines
longs for a cool breeze and for the soft arms
of a girl, he knows in San Francisco.

ON A VICTORY SHIP BOUND FOR SAIGON

The 12 to 4 watch,
it's 3 in the morning.
I finish pumping bilges
and secure the old steam pump.
It's time to make my round
back aft to check the steering gear.
I climb the ladder up through the fiddley,
all the way up to the main deck.
When I open the fiddley door,
hot engine room air rushes
out behind me, pushing me
and the door out into the alleyway.
To close the door, I push with all my weight.
When the door snaps shut, the metallic whine
of the turbine drops to a muffled hum.
I lay a flashlight beam
across the darkened afterdeck, just long enough
to mark my path, then shut it off.
Through the dark, I make my way across the deck.
There is no moon, but Venus sparkles so bright and big
I can see how it could be taken for a UFO.
And the Milky Way shines
like a glowing gas cloud across the sky.

At the fantail, I go below to check the gear.
A large electric motor turns on and off,
making adjustments on the rudder:
hummm click hummm click.
I go back up to the fantail and stand
at the railing. I light a cigarette
and look over the side. The sea is black,

and upon it, the ship's wake
is a boiling, phosphorescent path.
There is something about it that is strangely
inviting. I think of Hart Crane
climbing over the fantail rail in midday
and jumping, never to come up.
I look at my watch. It's getting late.
I take a long drag on my cigarette,
give it a flip, and watch it arc
down to the water like a shooting star.
I turn on my flashlight
and walk with hurried steps toward midship.
It's time now to call out
the 4 to 8 watch.

ON THE HOOK OFF KO SI CHANG

On the hook
off the island of Ko Si Chang.
On deck the heavy tropical heat
and the whine and groan
of cargo winches
hauling up sacks
of cassava flour from barges—
cassava flour for making tapioca.
White dust covers the deck
and cakes white on the sweaty bodies
of the half-naked stevedores.
They appear made up
to perform some primitive,
arcane ritual.

A young deckhand
stands on the railing
of the ship's bridge.
He waves down to me,
then dives in a long rainbow arc
into the turquoise water.
A few minutes later, a loud commotion
from the stevedores on the barge,
and the cargo winches go silent.
They've spotted a shark.
The deckhand kicks full-out
for the gangway.
I watch a lone shark fin
circle the ship.

The smiling deckhand
leaves wet footprints
in the white cassava dust.
The cargo winches start whining again.
All is back to normal.

At supper that evening, the cook,
having a diabolical sense of humor,
serves tapioca pudding
for dessert.

THE MESSMAN

Paranagua, Brazil. High on rum and Coke
and satiated with hot whorehouse sex, I walk
past the pounding music and loud argument
coming from the waterfront bar.
I walk through the big gate of the chain-link fence,
into the dark quarter of a mile
down to the dock and the Mormacmar,
scheduled to sail within the hour.
The waterfront is quiet,
the cargo loaded,
the stevedores gone.

I'm halfway to the ship,
and I hear a voice yelling,
"That's him! that's him there!"
I stop and watch a guard running toward me.
I wait for him. Breathing hard, he says,
"You owe money."
And I say, "No, I don't owe money."
Drawing his pistol and dropping to a crouch, smiling,
his white teeth shining in the semidarkness, he says,
"Yes, Señior, you owe money. Come, you pay."
Looking down the barrel of his pistol,
I was in no position to argue.

He walks me back to the waterfront bar. Jack,
our Messman, is standing outside the bar,
the bar's owner standing next to him;
big smile on Jack's big face.
His real name is Mervin,
but everyone calls him Jack. He looks

just like Jack Dempsey, and he has the build
to go with it. "Hey, kid," Jack says,
"you gotta pay my bar bill. I'm runnin' short."
Just then, we hear a long blast from the ship's whistle.
"Come on," says Jack, "don't fuck around or
we'll both miss the ship and maybe go to jail,
to boot." And the bar's owner says,
"Someone must pay, or you go to jail."
The guard has his hand on his pistol.

For any other shipmate, I'd pay without question,
but Jack has a history of intimidation,
often by brute force.
I really didn't care what they did with Jack.
But I pay his bar bill to save my own ass.
Walking back to the ship, Jack comes on nice.
"Don't worry, kid, I'll make it good
next draw when we make Santos."

As I well knew, Jack doesn't pay up,
and I don't ask him to.
One thing you learn aboard ship:
a smart seaman doesn't make an enemy
of the Messman, for he can do things to you
that you don't even want to think about.

THE VIEW FROM BELOW THE GUTTER

You know, when you hear a song or a piece
of music and it takes you back to a time in your past—
our psychologists have a name for this.
Well, right now I'm listening to something on the radio.
I don't know what it is, but it's so
mournful, a dark gloom has come over me,
and I find myself in that damp basement room
on Ellis Street in the San Francisco Tenderloin.
One room and a pantry-like kitchen that I rented
between ships during my sea-going days.
Standing up, looking out the small, barred window,
I was eye level with the sidewalk. I could only see
the people walking by from the knees down.
For someone to look into my room,
they'd have to get down on their hands and knees.
I once stared into the face of a man
picking up a cigarette butt. I remember
he smiled at me with most of his teeth missing.
Other than the landlord, he was the only one
that knew I was there.
Living below street level, you become aware
of the different sounds of people walking:
the tap tap tap of high heels, the thud, the clunk,
the cush, the clap, and the shuffle of different shoes
and the different ways that people walk.
After a while, I recognized certain people,
what they looked like from the knees down
and the sound they made when they walked.
I could overhear conversations, dialogs, and monologs,
shady deals being made, cries of desperation;
and one night, an armed robbery taking place.

Heard from below the gutter, all street sounds
were amplified: the sound of engines, the sound
of tires on the pavement, and when it rained, those tires
made a sizzling sound like potatoes dropped in hot grease.
After 6 weeks in that room, I was starting to feel
like a different species—troglodyte or moleman comes to mind.
But shipping was good, and I caught a Matson ship,
the Fleetwood, bound for Midway, Midway where
a big battle took place, and the gooney birds go to breed.

That dreadful music is over. They go to a commercial.
The man is hawking a pill that can change my life.
I think it's time to change the station.

A FEW MINUTES OF SOLITUDE

Somewhere below the equator,
headed for the Philippines,
I step through the fiddley door,
drenched in sweat
from the 110-degree heat
of the engine room.
It's 4 in the afternoon,
one hour till suppertime.
I go to my fo'c'sle and get a cool
can of beer from my ice chest.
I take my beer to the shade
of the starboard deck
and sit on a bench, alone.
There is no wind, only a hint
of a breeze made by the ship
as it slips through the water
at 15 knots.
I can hear the deckhands
chipping paint up near the bow.
I'm aware of the muffled groan
of the turbine deep below the waterline.
The ship, cutting the water,
makes a steady sound of ssh ssh.
The surface of the sea is smooth like ice,
shiny till it meets
the blue dome of the sky.
I take a long pull on my beer.
My wet clothes suck my body cool.
A school of flying fish breaks
the mirrored surface of the water
and the winged-fish glide glide glide;

then hit the bright skin of water and skip
like the flat rocks I used to throw
when I was a kid.
I try to remember ever seeing
a flying fish take flight
in choppy water. I can't.
I guess they are fair-weather fliers.
The chipping has stopped up forward;
the deckhands have knocked off.
I finish my beer and head for the shower.
After that, it will be
suppertime.

THE COLOMBO HOTEL, NORTH BEACH

I stayed at the Colombo Hotel
because it was cheap, and the location
convenient—not too far from the union hall
where I was trying to catch a ship.

The Colombo had a wide staircase
and spacious hallways, like the architect
was trying for elegance; then forgot
about it when he got to the rooms.

For the rooms were small, just big enough
for a bed, a chest of drawers with mirror,
and a washbasin in the corner.
A bare light bulb dangled from the ceiling.

My room had green woodwork and
beige wallpaper, peeling in spots.
In the brown stains on the ceiling,
I could make out landscapes,
strange faces and armies on the march.

The lobby where mostly old men sat
was furnished with a sagging, overstuffed
sofa, and a matching overstuffed chair.
There was a big window which always needed cleaning.

The big window looked out on Broadway.
The people passing looked in the window
like they were looking at animals in a zoo,
which wasn't too far from the truth.

Just when I thought the Colombo
had nothing to offer but drabness and gloom,
I discovered, down the hall, next to the toilet,
the door leading up to the roof.

On warm sunny days, when I wasn't at the union hall,
I would go up to the roof, take off my shirt,
and soak up the sun, read, and write
love letters to a woman in Vera Cruz.

But mostly I just sat there and took in the view.
All of central San Francisco
surrounded by the hills—
all the hills,
from Russian to Potrero, Nanny Goat to Nob.

The only skyscraper on the skyline—
Ma Bell's white terra-cotta tower
with the flag flying at its top.
A building worthy of its space in the sky.

The shiny, silver swoop of the Bay Bridge cables.
Freighters docked at the piers,
their booms out, loading and unloading cargo.
On Front Street, the bustling Produce Market.

No one ever joined me up there on the roof.
It was like the Colombo was peopled by
troglodytes afraid to leave their cave.
And I felt no need to enlighten them.

I was happy to have the Colombo's
one an only amenity all to myself.

Love In Many Ways

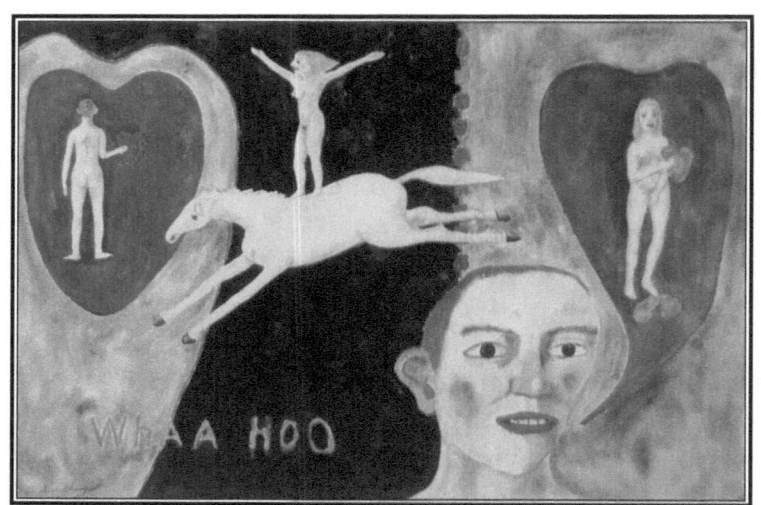

VERACRUZ

Slivers of moonlight
streaming through bamboo shades
the soft heat of her body
against mine
from the harbor the long moan of a ship's whistle
I light a cigarette
and take a sip of tequila
I listen to her breathing
each breath like a sigh
as she lies sleeping next to me

ARRIVEDERCI ROMA

After a long day at the union hall
where I'd been waiting for a ship,
I was walking through the financial district,
headed to my hotel room in North Beach,
when it started to rain. I ducked into a nearby
bar, sat on a stool and ordered a beer.
I looked at the woman sitting on the stool
next to me. She was a looker.
"You just get off work?" I asked.
"That I did," she said.
"What do you do?" I asked.
She gave me a bored look and said,
"I go up and down."
"You go up and down?" I repeated.
"Up and down—all day," she said.
She opened her blue eyes wider and smiled.
"I'm the last of the elevator operators," she said.
"You thought I was a hooker, didn't you?"
"It never crossed my mind," I lied.
"Come Friday, it's all over," she said.
"They're doing away with all of us."

She said her name was Roma.
She drank old-fashioneds, and I bought her one.
I had another beer, and we talked.
She told me how much she would miss
going up and down in her elevator.
And I said, "Don't worry, something else will turn up."
"You don't understand," she said.
"I don't want to do anything else."

We left the bar together, and that was the
beginning of our relationship—
a relationship that had its ups and downs.

Roma drew her unemployment and drank old-fashioneds.
And I spent my days at the union hall waiting
for a ship that never seemed to come.
Finally, one did—a ship on the jungle run.
I said good-bye to Roma and told her
I would write, which I did. I never got
an answer. I wasn't surprised, but I was disappointed.

When I got back from the jungle, I tried to find Roma.
No luck. Until one night in the Tenderloin
I saw her standing on the corner of Eddy and Taylor.
She was wearing a mini miniskirt.

I watched her from a distance. Soon
a man approached her; they talked.
Then they walked up Taylor Street together.

Well, I thought, as I walked off into the Tenderloin night,
in her own way, Roma is still
going up and down.

A DOG'S LIFE

We had been living together
for maybe a year.
Things were good between us.
Then she brought home a dog—
a big German shepherd.
Fine, I like dogs,
and this dog liked me.
He liked her even more.
But he was ready to make a meal
of anybody else.
That is to say, the dog was vicious.
I said You must get rid of him.
She refused. We argued.
I said It's me or the dog.
Soon after that ultimatum, I came home,
and the dog was gone.
We did not talk about it.
Life returned to its pre-dog smoothness.
A month went by. Then one afternoon,
she walked in with the dog on a leash.
When she saw the look on my face
she said, Don't worry, don't worry,
I had him castrated.
As it turned out,
the dog was meaner than ever.

And so were the arguments.

When I started packing my things,
she said, No, wait, I'll get him a muzzle.
It was then I knew for sure
I had to get out of there.
I saw in what direction we were headed.

I did not want to lose my
balls.
And I've always hated
muzzles.

TWO TREES MAKING LOVE

I'm sitting in a little café
on Church Street
drinking coffee and
watching two trees making love.
It's true. One tree looks female
and the other tree looks male.
The male tree has a larger trunk
than the female,
and he has a scruffier head
of leaves. He's also
slightly taller.
The female tree has a delicate look,
and she has a well-groomed
head of leaves.
There is a slight breeze blowing,
and the way the leafy heads
of the male and female come
together, it looks as if
they are kissing. And when
the breeze picks up, it appears
as though they are doing
other things.
From where I sit, watching
these two trees in the throes
of passion is quite a show.
This is hot stuff.
If the wrong people
find out about this,
they'll have those trees
chopped down.

Anyway, when I finish my coffee,
I think I'll go home
and see what mood
Ellen's in.

UNION
For Ellen

An old clay pot
full of rich dirt
waits in the hot sun
for seed and water.

Under the porch
a mud dauber works
at building a nest.

A ship nearing port
after a long voyage
sounds its horn.

Somewhere in the city
a whore smiles
as she takes the money
from her john.

In the forest
a hunter draws a bead
on an unsuspecting deer.

In Saint Paul's Cathedral
on the corner
a priest takes confession
from a thief.

And I sit here in this room
with the shades drawn
listening to good music
and thankful I found you
when I did.

Memories and Musings: Personal

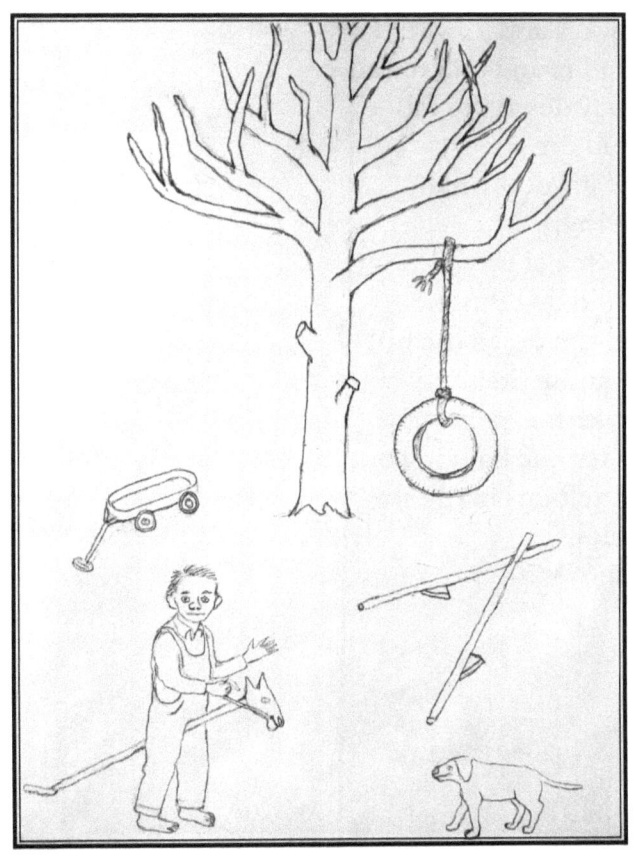

AS THE WORLD TURNS

Yes, I know
it's an old soap opera.
But it's also me
7 years old
all folded up
inside an old rubber tire
rolling down a hill,
seeing the world
up, sideways and down
up, sideways and down
up, sideways and down
round and round and round
all the way down the hill
till the old tire
comes to a wobbly halt
and I lie there
too dizzy to get up
and my old dog Buster,
who had run down the hill
barking at the tire,
stands over me, panting
with his tongue hanging out
while the clouds in the sky
turn in slow
circles above me.

PULLING UP ROOTS

my father
& industrial-strength religion
a call for confrontation
i pull up my roots early
& try to find my way
i choose the uneasy freedom
of the renegade & the nonbeliever
i study the lessons taught
far from home
i learn the bad smell
of a sweet deal
gone sour
& i'm not fooled by
prime time temptation
i ride out ugly times
i try to hone the finer points
of getting by
but the man who lives free
doesn't always prosper
the forbidding terrain of freedom
often hides calamity
i am caught
in a circle of woes
still looking for answers
a wild sheep
in a land of tough outlaws
i rage against memory
and the peril of forgetting
i search
for a less burdensome path
perhaps even a touch
of home

THE HEIFER

As we crossed the pasture of waving yellow grass,
I could see the lone live oak tree,
the windmill and the watering trough.
As we drew nearer, I could see
the downed heifer lying near the tree.

That morning my father had said, "You'll stay home
from school today. There's a heifer down,
and I need your help." I was 8 years old
and more than happy to stay home from school,
especially with my father's blessing.

My father backed up the old Ford pickup
close to the heifer. I could see 2 small black hooves
protruding from the heifer's swollen backside.
The heifer raised her head and bawled, strings
of saliva hanging from her mouth.

A wild look in her eye as she strained
to extrude the calf inside of her.
"She can't do it by herself," my father said.
"We'll have to give her a little help."
Then he told me to get the wire stretchers.

He tied a soft cotton rope to the little calf legs
and attached the rope to the wire stretchers.
Then he hooked the stretchers to the pickup's bumper.
"When I tell you to pull," he said, "you pull.
And when I tell you to stop, you lock the stretchers."

The young heifer lifted her head
as if trying to see the source of her pain;
in her eye, a look of helpless fear.

She bawled and pushed, and a few more inches
of her calf's legs appeared, and my father said, "pull!"

And slowly, as I pulled on the stretchers,
and my father worked with his hands
the newborn calf emerged all slick and wet.
My father cut the umbilical cord
and wiped the calf clean with a gunny sack.

Then he rolled up his sleeve
and reached inside the heifer,
up past his elbow.
He told me he had to do it—
to clean out all of the afterbirth,
for the heifer could not do it on her own.

When he was satisfied that the heifer was clean,
my father and I got her on her feet.
And for the first time, she got a look
at that little thing that had caused her so much pain.
She gave a long moo of relief, or maybe joy.

Then she began to lick her wobbly newborn calf.
My father had me take a shovel
and bury the afterbirth while he
washed at the watering trough.
Before we left, the calf had found its mother's tit.

On the way home my father said,
"Son, I couldn't have done it without you."
I knew that wasn't true. I think he kept me
out of school to teach me about pain and suffering
and, above all, the miracle of life.

ON THE WAY TO MY MOTHER'S FUNERAL

At the airport
walking down a long corridor
I'm shocked to see my dead father
walking toward me;
so shocked am I that I say out loud, "Oh, my God!"
Then I see that it is only my reflection
in a large mirror.
Until that moment, I had not realized
how much I had become my father,
and in that moment I understand
why the tension between us.
I see what my father had always seen:
He saw himself in me,
and he could never approve of what he saw.
Don't let the kid get the better of you—
competition, not approval,
my father's approach to raising a son.
He was a righteous man, a preacher, a man of God,
and in those things he had me bested.
I was the rebel, the wanderer, the profligate,
and in those things I had him bested.
We had a real good game going;
the more righteous he became,
the more I became the rebel.
This contest lasted for years,
until I got married,
then we both called time out.
But right up to the end, I was the itch
he could not scratch.

I reach the end of the corridor,
take a last look at myself in the mirror,
turn left and take the escalator up
to catch the plane to my mother's funeral.

ASYMMETRY

It's comforting to know
that nature is asymmetrical.
Physicists tell us
that if nature were symmetrical,
matter and antimatter would be equal,
which would mean they would
destroy each other.
And that would have meant
the end of the world before it even got started.
So nature, by its nature,
is a little out of kilter.
Which brings me to my face,
a face that goes beyond asymmetrical;
it is downright lopsided.
If nature were anything like my face,
we would all be in trouble.
God knows, my face
has caused me enough trouble.
How many times have I had to either run or fight
because someone said, "I don't like your face!"
And when I was young,
before I took on the harmless look of age,
the cops used to stop me
for no apparent reason.
Something about my uneven look
aroused their suspicion.

They would question me,
then reluctantly let me go.
And I can't say that I blame them,
for after all these years
of looking at my face,
I'm still a little suspicious
myself.

FIRST CUP OF TEA

Tree leaves shimmer
with early morning sunlight.
The Chinese painters
are just starting work
on the house next door.
They laugh and talk Chinese.
Their extension ladders
make a jarring, metallic clangor.
The almost inaudible sound
of piano music comes
from the radio in the kitchen.
It's 8 o'clock—8 bells
and somewhere merchant seamen
are changing watch.
Anchovies swim in an endless circle
under the lights in Monterey.
A motorboat coughs and sputters.
Somewhere a woman with a basket on her head
opens her arms to the day.
And a bamboo grasshopper
is trying to take flight.
A sweaty boxer smiles,
revealing a white mouthpiece.
And an earth-red goddess of fertility
leans against a white plaster wall.
Several days of newspapers
are scattered on the floor.
The teakettle in the kitchen
begins to whistle.
The piano music still plays—
something by Schubert, I think.

I pour the boiling water.
A big world, a small world.
I return to my place
on the old couch.
I sip my first cup of tea.

And the house next door
gets a new coat of paint.

I SHOULD WRITE A POEM

Today is such a beautiful Spring day.
I feel guilty for not writing a poem about it.
I should tell you how just today the old apple tree
in the backyard exploded with pink-white blossoms.
I should tell you about the lemons
hanging on the tree-like little suns.
I should tell you how the wooden fisherman
slowly paddles his boat in the gentle breeze.
I should tell you about the heavy drone
of hungry bees.
I should tell you about the happy splashing
of blue jays in the birdbath.
I should tell you about the row of pink
underpants hanging on the clothesline
soaking up the dazzling sunshine.

Yes, I think I should write a poem about it.

6 STREET NOTE #1

i saw a book
in the gutter
pages fluttering
like a butterfly
like angel wings
beckoning
i picked it up
dirt-smeared Rimbaud
i sat in sunny doorway
reading
serendipity on the
ugly 6

SNAPSHOT OF SID

As I look out the window
a slow drizzle is falling.
It's been raining for 3 days now
and gloom has set in.
Right now I feel used and worthless
like the old furniture
my mother moved from house to house.
To break my funk
I decide to walk to the bank
and make a withdrawal—
a little extra cash to raise my spirits.
On my way, I pass a pile of rubble
strewn around a ruptured cardboard box,
soggy-wet and sagging in on itself.
It looks as if a hungry dog
had pawed through this box of discards
looking for a nonexistent morsel of food.
I stand there under my umbrella
as the rain slowly falls, looking at this collection
of disconnected junk: a naked rag doll
with one leg missing, lying face down
with its stubby arms spread wide
as though trying to hug the sidewalk;
a greasy green couch pillow, one corner ripped open,
cotton stuffing scattered about like dirty snow;
a shiny brass doorknob;
a paperback book with cover missing;
3 copies of Ladies Home Journal.
I look inside the box: a tossed salad
of old wet clothes.

But next to a lady's brown glove
a yellowed snapshot. I pick it up.
A young man wearing a fedora
and a 1930's suit
leans with one arm against a telephone pole.
He has a wide, cocky smile on his face,
as if to say, "Look at me,
I'm holding up a telephone pole."
The desert stretches behind him.
In the foreground, the shadow
of the woman taking the picture.
I turn the picture over.
On the back, written in pencil: "Sid in the desert."
And stamped in faded purple ink:
BEAR FOTO, 1939.

I put the snapshot in my pocket
and continue on to the bank.
I make my withdrawal and head home.
I pass the pile of junk. Nothing has changed
except the brass doorknob is missing.
OK, someone got the brass doorknob.
They can sell the brass to the junkman
or use the doorknob to open a door.
But I have Sid's snapshot
and I'm going home
and make up the story
of Sid's life.

SLOW DAY AT THE STORE

Not a customer in sight,
and time hangs in the air like drying fish.
The Muzak oozes
through the warehouse rafters,
and to jump-start the day,
I dance down the aisle
of plumbing paraphernalia.
I fox-trot past the P-traps,
jitterbug by the J-bends,
and tango through the fittings.
I quickstep to the plungers,
then waltz around the piping
with a plumber's helper in my arms.
And I'm thinking Kelly and Astaire.

Then from behind me, over the Muzak,
I hear the manager's voice:
"What's the matter? Are you having a seizure?"
What an insult, I think.
 Couldn't he see I was dancing?
"No, sir," I say. "I'm OK,
 just trying to shake out some kinks."
"Are you sure?" he says.
 You had me worried there for a while."
And I wonder how long he'd been watching me.
"It's a slow day," the manager says.
"So why don't you just take it easy."
Truly an understanding boss.
I go to my workbench
and start writing on a notepad.
What the hell... if I can't dance
I'll write a poem.

ON THE OLD ROAD

A clear November morning
two hours past sunrise.
A chill in the air
and his breath fogs up
as he sits on his horse
and rolls a Bull Durham cigarette.
He's 16 years old,
a high school dropout
working for the Crofton Cattle Ranch.
He's making his daily 15-mile circle
of the different pastures,
feeding hay to hungry cattle.

He's riding on what used to be
the highway over the Tehachapi Pass.
He's stopped at a point on the old road
where every morning he takes a break,
rolls his cigarette, smokes,
looks out over the grassy foothills
and beyond to the San Joaquin Valley
and the town of Bakersfield
in the hazy distance.

At the time, he does not know this,
but it's the same spot where
the Joad family of Grapes of Wrath
stopped and looked out on
the promised land.
Something else he does not know:
he does not know that he will look back
on this time as the one time in his life
when he knew exactly what he wanted to do
and he was doing it.

THE BULLFIGHT

At the Plaza de Toros, Guadalajara
I have the choice of sol or sombra—sun or shade.
I choose the seats in the sun;
   they are cheaper, and I'll be sitting with the people.
The sun is warm and the beer is cold
and the novilleros are fighting today.
Novilleros—apprentice bullfighters—
anything can happen and will.
I'm sitting between two men, both taking
nips from their bottles of tequila.
The man on my left wears a floppy felt hat.
He's grim in manner with a blind right eye.
He turns and looks at me with an eye as white as milk.
The man on my right wears a straw sombrero.
He's small and dark with two bright eyes,
and his teeth sparkle white when he smiles.
The trumpet sounds, and the toreros
march in wearing their glimmering suits of light.
Homage is paid to some big shot in the stands.
Then the bullfight begins.
Three novilleros will fight two bulls apiece.
The first bull outdrives his horns into the belly
of the picador's horse. The horse goes down.
But he gets up and staggers from the bullring.
The one-eyed man yells, "Pendejo!" at the picador—
stupid for letting the bull gore the horse.

The little man on my right says in English,
"You Americano, no?"
I answer yes, and he offers me a drink
of his tequila, which I take.

Then he says, "You know Marysville?"
And I say, "Yes, I know Marysville."
He offers me another hit of tequila
and says, "I picka peaches in Marysville."
And I say, "My father also picked peaches in Marysville,"
which happens to be the truth.
And the little man beams as if he has found a soul mate.

In the bullring, the new novillero is doing
a smooth, clean job of fighting his bull.
The one-eyed man is yelling, "Que bueno! Que bueno!"
Then the novillero goes in for the kill,
and he executes a masterpiece.
The one-eyed man yells, "Bravo! Bravo!"
The crowd yells, "Bravo! Bravo!"
And the novillero is awarded the bull's ears.
I buy the little man and me a bottle of beer.
The fights continue from mediocre to bad.
The one-eyed man is yelling, "Cabron! Cabron!"
and sometimes, "Chinga madre!"
The little man and I drink our beers
and nip from his bottle of tequila.
I'm feeling warm—warm from the sun
and warm from the glow of tequila in my gut.
The little man raises his bottle and says,
"To Marysville, salud," and takes a hit,
hands me the bottle, and I say, "To picking peaches."
And the little man says, "Si, si, to picka peaches."
The novillero who was awarded the ears
is fighting his second bull, and he's having
a terrible time. Nothing is going right,
and his time is running out.
People are throwing bottles and half-eaten

burritos into the bullring.
The one-eyed man is yelling, "Hijo de puta!
Hijo de puta! Matalo!"
"Son of a whore! Kill him!"
The little man and I are smiling at the spectacle.
The novillero fails to kill his bull.
In one afternoon, he has known triumph and disgrace.

When the bullfight ends, I shake the little man's hand,
thank him for the tequila, and we say good-bye.
As I leave, the one-eyed man looks at me
with his good eye, smiles and says, "Adios."
I leave the Plaza de Toros in the sundown light
and go in search of some tortillas, rice, and beans
to smother the tequila, fire burning in my belly.

HORSEPOWER

These days, when people think
of horsepower,
they're apt to think
Jaguar, Mustang,
Chevy, GTO, etc.
But to truly appreciate
horsepower,
you must, as I have,
walk behind
a well-matched team
of horses
pulling a heavy, punishing
load up a hill.
You keep the lines tight,
so the horses know
you are in charge.
You talk to them.
You call out their names:
"Major, Fuquay, dig in boys!"
And they hunker down.
They fart, they dig.
It's a thing of beauty.
It's horsepower.

CROWS

I'm always startled
to hear the caw
of a crow
in the city.
It always takes me back
to hot summer sun
on green cornfields,
old fences, buzzing insects,
dusty dirt roads and bare feet.
Somehow I feel that crows
don't belong in the city.
And sometimes I feel
I don't either.

On Time and Aging

OF TIME AND THE LEAKY FAUCET
An Installation by Paul Kos

A grandfather clock,
some 10 feet tall,
wood stained dark, stands
against the white plaster wall.
The hands and numbered face
are missing. In their place,
2 dripping water cocks
mark the passing time:
  drip drop
  drip
  drip drop
  drip drop
    drop
  drip drop
  drip
The dripping water drops
down through the clock's
empty bowels,
landing in a hidden pool
and echoing with a wet, hollow plunk.

Suddenly, I saw it true.
Time does not flow
like the sun from east to west,
or like the hands around the clock's face.
Time does not march
1-2-3-4,
nor does it flow like a river.

True, time sometimes flies
like a crazed bat,
but mostly, it drips.
Time drips through the mind
like a leaky faucet.

SIX HAIKU

Lunch—sidewalk cafe
people pass by in the sun
I am so hungry.

A boy kicks a can
old sneakers hang from power line
memories rush by.

The wind is blowing
the weather vane is spinning
going nowhere fast.

The alarm goes off
my warm feet hit the cold floor
a new day begins.

How quickly spring came
the apple tree exploded
with blossoms today.

Warm summer evening
the sound of passing traffic
lonely motel room.

YOUTH

he is young and youth is not burdened
with the guilt of wasted beauty

it is youth who rides the surf
of this tragic sea

it is youth who finds egregious error
often ends in orchids

youth has no age

age never dims the diamond's shine

you are never too old
to be young

MY FATHER-IN-LAW'S EYES

He's only sixteen, but he looks forty.
He stares down at me
from his photograph hanging on the wall—
a shoulder and head snapshot.
He's wearing the uniform
of a private in the Greek Army.
His furious black eyes stare down at me
like a deadly double-barreled
weapon zeroed in on a target.

These are the eyes
that watched his father die
of exhaustion on the death march to the Syrian desert
during the Armenian genocide.
The Turkish soldiers kept saying,
"Keep moving! Keep moving!"
until it became a mantra.

These are the eyes
that watched his mother die
of starvation in Mosul, Iraq.

These are the eyes
of a night fisherman on the black sea
who had a girlfriend named Panky.

These are the eyes
of a trucker who made runs from Iraq to Iran.

These are the eyes
of a man who spent nineteen months
in a Baghdad prison for manslaughter.

These are the eyes
of a man who had six years of schooling
but spoke eight languages.

These are the eyes
of a man who had a paint store on Haight Street
in the Haight-Ashbury district of San Francisco.

These are the eyes
of a man who befriended the hippies.
He would give them a handout, then tell them,
"Keep moving, keep moving."

THE CUSTOMER

I've spent my life traveling
the world
by ship, by plane, by car,
by thumb, by horse, and
even a short way,
by camel.

Now, here I am
come to roost
in the plumbing department
of Discount Builder's Supply.

I'm standing here
in my khaki pants
and dirty blue apron.
It's a slow, hot Sunday afternoon.
The customers have been few
and mean.
(It's difficult to be happy
when the plumbing goes bad.)

A young woman
in a miniskirt
comes toward me down the aisle.
I straighten up and
pull my shoulders back.

"Perhaps you can help me," she says.
"Perhaps I can," I say.
"What seems to be your problem?"
"My toilet just keeps running
  and running. What should I do?"

"Sounds like your flapper
has gone bad," I say.
"Or could be you're ready
for a ballcock."

She looks at me;
her eyes get big.
"You're putting me on,
aren't you?" she says.

"No, Ms., I'm serious."
I walk her down the aisle
to the flappers.
"Here," I say. "Put on a new
one of these.
If that doesn't do the trick,
then come on back
and I'll fix you up
with a ballcock."

"Oh, thank you," she says.
And she smiles
and I watch her
walk down the aisle.

The flapper must have worked
for she doesn't return.

I spend the rest of the day
feeling like an old rooster
waiting for the dawn
so he can crow
one more time.

I SEE IT COMING

The wild stallion
of my youth
has turned into
a clumsy workhorse.

And what's that
coming down the road?
O Jesus! It's a stubborn
old mule.

OH, FRIZZLE DIZZLE DAZZLE & DIP

oh, frizzle dizzle dazzle and dip
give me some feedback give me some lip

follow your zigzag kiss your fate
bad things happen to those who wait

don't get stuck in time bound places
try to make love to all 3 graces

and just when life seems all hunky-dory
that's when you'll miss that last grab for glory

but that won't matter if you're cool if you're hip
oh, frizzle dizzle dazzle & dip

AS THE TELEPHONE RINGS

Death sits at the sewing machine
sewing a new black shroud

On Blue Mountain, a skull rests under a cross
between two unlit torches

An antique Remington typewriter
sits against a white wall collecting dust

A yellowed paper in the Remington
waits for someone to type a message

In India, the tourists on safari
fail to see the tiger slipping through the jungle

The telephone rings
and rings and rings

The torches on Blue Mountain
will never again be lit

The message will never be written
on the yellowed paper in the Remington

The tourists on safari will never
spy the tiger in the jungle

But smiling Death will be with us
dressed in his new black shroud

The telephone rings once more
then silence

Mysteries, Oddities, and Ironies -

Philosophic Reflections

ANGER IS NOT ENOUGH

anger is not enough
it's finally time for freedom
time to play
with wacky toys
fall under the influence
of an itch
go swimming in the nude
throw a Frisbee
watch the pigeons
shit on the flag
have a rendezvous
with a stranger
take the telephone
off the hook
mix a drink
read a book
or perhaps just sit
& think

EVIDENCE OF MY JOURNEY

In the coffeehouse,
two tables over, a young woman
is writing a postcard
with her left hand.
It occurs to me
that left-handed people
push the letters into existence
and right-handed people
pull the letters into being.
What can I conclude from this?
Not much. So I return
to the book I'm reading.

I remove the airline boarding pass
I'm using for a bookmark.
On the back of the pass
it says, NOTICE.
Please retain this stub
and your ticket receipt
as evidence of your journey.
Oh, I will, I will.
I shall also retain my twisted
nose and lined face
as further evidence of my journey.

As I open my book, the left-handed
woman leaves the coffeehouse,
leaving me thinking
left, right—push, pull.

HANGING ON

My grip is not as good as it used to be
But I'm still hanging on

Still trying to unravel the tricky
Meanings of life

The older I get, the more my past
Comes sneaking up on me

The past I can't shrug off
The future gets here ever faster

But if you want to make me laugh
Tell me it's time for seriousness

I can see the dark side of optimism
And the bright side of pessimism

The holy man becomes a monster
A thief, the caretaker of the treasure

Truth is always under pressure
And amid all the delicacy junk still reigns

But somewhere down an out-of-the-way road
The wildflowers are still in bloom

MOST OF US

Most of us, if we're lucky,
make it into adulthood.
We get a job, get married, have kids.
I was lucky enough
to accomplish two of the above.
But I never wanted
to have kids anyway.
How could I ever
explain it all to a child, especially one
that doesn't want to listen,
and when I myself am trying
to work out what's happening.

Most of us, lucky or unlucky,
never do anything spectacular.
We don't become famous or infamous,
nor do we become heroes.
Even if we are cursed with a yearning
for recognition or power,
we seldom, if ever, achieve either one.
What we are and who we are in the end
is the sum of small acts,
which is perhaps a blessing.

LINES OF THOUGHT
(From the drawings of William Kentridge)

A man in a black suit sits at his desk
The blue glow of a computer
The black telephone
The white leaves of a Rolodex
A breeze through the open window
Papers full of numbers rustle on his desk
He follows the blue lines of his thought
A nude woman in a tacky hotel room
A black cat leaps from the bed
An angry mob is forming in the street
A train passes through
He senses the nude standing behind him
She reaches to tap his shoulder
A blue line cuts her off
The black cat scurries across his desk
White papers full of black numbers go flying
The telephone rings
He answers, and a voice says, Give!
The line goes dead
He closes his eyes
The blue lines form a blue cat
The blue cat walks through the darkness
It watches him with yellow eyes
He is alone in the hotel room
He sits in a chair near the window
He can hear the mob in the street
He asks himself, What is it that they want?
The black cat sits at his feet
He looks at the walls covered with numbers—
Rubbed-out and corrected calculations

He looks at the clock on the wall
The red hand moves in one-second jumps
The nude stands behind him
She moves in close and runs her fingers through his hair
Again the telephone rings
He listens to it ring
And as it rings, he thinks:
Some things stay in the mind forever

MOTHER NATURE

Who was that first person
Who gave Mother Nature her name?
And what was he thinking?
It must have been a warm,
Sunny spring day with blossoming
Wildflowers filling the meadow.

Now, as I write this,
We have wildfires and floods,
Earthquakes and tsunamis,
Tornados, hurricanes,
And volcano eruptions.
All of them killing
Hundreds or thousands of people.

No mother would do such a thing
Unless she was out of her mind.
No. It is not a mother's nature.

QUESTION

Hello, God.
Are you there?
I'd like to ask you a question.
I don't expect an answer
but I'll ask it anyway.
Before that thing we call The Big Bang,
what was it like being all scrunched up
in that tiny point of buzzing matter?
And how did you happen to be
in such a fix?
It's quite understandable why you wanted
to break free of that dark, minuscule prison,
to flex your muscles, expand, spread yourself around.
But you've been expanding for a very long time.
Aren't you concerned that you'll spread yourself too thin?
So thin that you'll be only a wisp of yourself?
Maybe so thin and far away that our little world
will have to stumble along without you?
Judging from the way things down here are going,
maybe that's already happening.
According to the record, you used to speak
to us from time to time.
Have you drifted so far away from us
that we can no longer hear you?
Tell me this isn't so.
Tell me you haven't deserted us.

STRING THEORY

A popular theory
among physicists today
says that the building blocks
of matter are made up
of vibrating strings.
I like this theory—the universe
a big ball of strings,
and God a playful cat.

THE BUTTERFLY

This morning I set free
a monarch butterfly,
flapping its wings and beating its head
relentlessly against the windowpane.
I gently cupped it in my hands
and tossed it out the open window.

Wouldn't it be nice, I thought,
if sometimes there was some
big guy out there to cup us in his hands
and gently place us on the other side
of that brick wall we stubbornly
beat our heads against.

THUNDER AND LIGHTNING

We don't get much
thunder and lightning
in San Francisco.
But when we do,
it's usually a pleasant experience.

I can imagine
some ancient people
believing that thunder was
God speaking.

Thunder has many voices—
from low rumbles to
sky-splitting explosions
with lightning providing
the appropriate punctuation—
fleeting commas to
slashing exclamations.

Those ancient people
knew when God
was angry or open
to conversation.

Tonight, the thunder I hear
and the lightning I see
tell me that God is open
to conversation.
But I don't know
what to say.

TROUBLES

Most of our troubles
nothing but bubbles
that burst with sufficient airing.

MORNING WALK

The sun behind me
Long shadow in front of me
Pulling me along

THERE IS POWER IN THE MUD

O yes there is power, O yes there is power
O yes there is power in the mud

Now, Jesus had his Jordan and the Sea of Galilee
But I got the Mississippi for a muddy jubilee

Gonna crawl in that mud like a Loo-zee-ana gator
Gonna toot my horn like a fogbound freighter

Gonna spurt my spout like the big white whale
Gonna kick up my heels, that mud I'm gonna flail

Gonna cry HALLELUJAH with an earth-shakin' shout
Gonna praise that mud till my lungs give out

O yes there is power, O yes there is power
O yes there is power in the mud

Gonna dance the jig and listen to it spatter
Gonna cry SCREW YOU and what does it matter

I came from the mud, and to the mud, I return
The rest of the world ain't none of my concern

O you can take my blood, but you can't have my soul
So stand back, brother, in that mud I'm gonna roll

O yes there is power, O yes there is power
O yes there is power in the mud.

PART III
Short Stories

MEMORIES OF THE GREAT DEPRESSION

It was the middle of the Great Depression. I was five years old, and we were living in Amarillo, Texas. It was a long time ago, but I remember it clearly. It was a time that had a way of sticking in everybody's mind that had lived through it. Being the young kid that I was, I didn't face the hardships of the grown-ups. I was aware of the problems, but I thought that was just the way life was.

The only really bad thing I remember was the dust storms. They were truly frightening. We could see one coming from miles away, growing larger as it approached, a huge, black roiling cloud. We always hurried to seal off the cracks in the windows and doors, in a not very successful attempt to keep the dust out.

When the dust cloud arrived, it arrived with a hellish roar and a smothering blanket of dust and darkness. There was nothing we could do until it passed, but sit it out and breathe as best we could the dusty air filtered through a dampened handkerchief. We would listen to the creaking house, the rattling windows, and the wailing of the wind. Then, when this monstrous thing moved on, it left everything in the house covered with a layer of dust, which took the family several days to clean up.

Another memory that stands out in my mind is the many transient men who came to our house for a bite to eat. Our house was only a few blocks from the railroad tracks, and hardly a day went by that one, two, or three men would come knocking on our door, asking for something to eat. Our address had been passed along on the transient grapevine as a place where they would be sure to get a meal.

My mother always had a big pot of pinto beans on the stove, and she was an expert at cooking beans. To this day, I try to cook beans the way my mother did. I call them "beans a la momma." And there was always some kind of potatoes—fried, baked, or mashed—and potato salad, which she made from leftover mashed potatoes. The first time I ate potato salad made with chunks of potatoes, I thought there was something wrong with it.

And the bread, my mother made her own bread. For her, it was a physical workout, the way she kneaded and pounded that dough. Then she would put it into the pans, and I was amazed at how the dough would rise way up above the tops of the pans. Along with the bread, she would make one big pan of cinnamon rolls. I can't think of a more tantalizing aroma than the aroma coming from the oven as my mother's bread and rolls were baking.

So, along with the beans and potatoes and whatever else was available to put on a transient man's plate, my mother would include a big chunk of homemade bread. And when they finished that, there was always seconds.

The men would knock on our front door, and my mother would have them go around to our screened-in back porch. Some of these men were coming for their second and even third time and knew to go directly to the back porch. If my father was home, they were invited to sit at the kitchen table. These men were not bums. They were just men on the move, looking for work.

My mother would have been happy running a boarding-house; she really missed her calling. She liked feeding these men. I think she was disappointed if several days passed without a knock on our door.

I used to stand around and watch the men eat, and my mother would say, "Now, Buck, don't bother the gentleman while he's eating."

Buck was my nickname. Buck Jones, the movie cowboy, was my hero, and I insisted that everyone call me Buck. I was usually in character with my holster and pistol strapped on my hip.

My mother always asked the men where they were headed, and most of the time, they said California.

Soon after my sixth birthday, my father lost his job at the Great West Mill, and we too packed up and headed for California.

I started my first school year in Marysville. Some of the kids called me Okie, and I said, "I'm no Okie. I come from Texas."

So, they started calling me Tex. Now I had two nicknames. With Tex as a moniker, I climbed up a rung or two on their ladder of esteem, just high enough that they stopped calling me Okie.

But most of all, what I've often thought about is those disappointed transient men who knocked on our door after we had left for California.

BUSTER AND TOM

When I was a kid, around 8 years old, I lived outside Marysville, CA, between the Feather River and Plumas Lake. The lake has since been pumped dry, but at that time, it was a fine little lake with lots of catfish, ducks, and even a colony of beavers. The beavers had built their dam across a narrow channel that connected the two sections of the lake.

Although our house was nothing more than a three-room shack, for an 8-year-old, this place was paradise. I swam in the river, made my own raft and sailed it on the lake, and played Tarzan in the jungles surrounding the lake.

It was at this time that my father brought home a dog, which we named Buster. Buster had the markings of a collie but none of the collie's sleekness, the sharp nose, or the long hair. Buster was obviously a mixture of what we didn't know, nor did we care.

About that same time, we acquired a cat, a big gray tomcat. I don't know where the cat came from, whether someone brought the cat home, or whether he just turned up one day. We called the cat Tom, or if we were being affectionate, Kitty Tom.

Buster became my constant companion. We went everywhere together. When I went swimming in the river, so did Buster, and when I sailed my homemade raft, he came with me. If my mother saw the dog and I was nowhere around, she would get worried and say to him: "Buster, where's Buck? Go find Buck." And off Buster would go, barking and running straight to where I was.

For a year or more, Buster and Tom seemed to have a normal dog-cat relationship. Buster went his way, and Tom went his.

It wasn't that they avoided each other. It was more like they ignored one another's existence.

Then one day, Buster and I came home from a trip to the river, and we found Tom sleeping under the front steps. This was unusual because the front steps were Buster's territory; the space under the steps was Buster's doghouse. He had an old blanket under there to sleep on, and his bowl, where we fed him our dinner scraps, was nearby.

I had never seen Tom under those steps before. Tom would climb up the steps to get into the house the few times my mother would let him in, but never under them. Yet, there he was all curled up on Buster's blanket, purring away. And surprisingly, Buster didn't seem bothered by Tom's encroachment into his territory. He looked under the porch, sniffed around, then turned his attention to me as if to say: "Well, what are we going to do now?"

After that, it became such a common thing to see Tom lying on Buster's blanket that I wasn't surprised when I saw Buster and Tom lying on the blanket together. It was clear that Buster was no longer the sovereign under the steps; he was sharing his house and blanket with Tom now.

Tom was a hunter, much more so than Buster. Buster would give short chase to some creature if he happened upon it, but he would soon give up. Buster didn't have that killer instinct like Tom. Tom brought home all sorts of small animals and varmints: cotton-tail rabbits, squirrels, rats, mice, birds, and once, he came trotting in with a snake in his mouth, the tail dragging three or four feet behind him. Tom deposited all his kill under the porch. Some he ate, and some, like cottontails and squirrels, Buster would eat. But mostly they would just lay there and rot. It was my job to keep things cleaned up.

One day the man who was mowing a nearby field of alfalfa came to our house and asked us if we owned a big gray cat. We told him we did. He said he was sorry, but he thought it might have gotten caught in the mower blades. He said it must have been lying in the tall alfalfa, and he couldn't see it. He heard a squeal and saw the cat jump high, trailing blood, and by the time he got his team of horses stopped, the cat was gone. He told us again how sorry he was and that he would keep an eye out for our cat.

The whole family was devastated. We all loved that cat. Buster and I spent days combing the countryside, looking for Kitty Tom's body. We found a bloody trail leading for a short way through the alfalfa field; then it disappeared, and we could never find another trace of him.

Buster seemed to spend less time under the porch. He went off on his own more than in the past. Maybe he was looking for Kitty Tom, or maybe he knew things weren't the same, and he just didn't know what to do about it. My mother, who used to say "Buster, where's Buck?" was now saying, "Buck, where's Buster?"

A month or so passed, and we had all resigned ourselves to Kitty Tom's death. We were even talking about getting another cat. Then, early one morning, I heard Buster barking. I ran out the front door, and Kitty Tom was standing there on three legs. Half his right hind leg was missing, and he was so skinny he was nothing but matted hair and bone. Buster was beside himself. He ran in circles; then, he would jump on me, then run some more.

My mother opened a big can of tuna and fed Kitty Tom, and we all stood around and silently watched him eat his first good meal since the accident.

How did he survive all that time on his own with an amputated leg? I don't know. But, I do know cats have a strong instinct for survival. Often when they get sick, they will go off by themselves and eat certain grasses that have curative powers. Kitty Tom was most definitely a cat with strong instincts.

For the next few weeks, Kitty Tom got the royal treatment. Instead of leftovers from our table, which is what he and Buster usually got, my mother bought him canned tuna and salmon, and even some cat food. For my mother, this was pushing the envelope of magnanimity. She was never one to mollycoddle animals.

In what seemed like no time at all, Kitty Tom gained back most of the weight he had lost, and his coat had become slick and shiny again. He was able to get around amazingly well on his three legs. Though he wasn't the hunter he once was, he still brought home a rat or mouse occasionally.

Since Kitty Tom's return, his relationship with Buster had changed. Before, their relationship was one of friendly toleration; but now, they seemed to be more like buddies, at least as much as a dog and cat can be. Once I saw them both under the porch, sleeping. Kitty Tom was lying all curled up in Buster's flank. When I went into the house, I tiptoed up the front steps because I didn't want to disturb them.

The next spring, the owner of a large farm nearby decided to exterminate the squirrels on his property. He had men riding around on horseback, throwing poison grain into all the squirrel holes they could find. At the time, we didn't realize what the consequences of this would be. But the terrible realization was all too soon in coming.

One warm Sunday evening, when we returned from church services, we found Buster stretched out in the driveway. I jumped out of the car and ran up to him. When I touched him, he was already stiff. I stood there in the car's headlights, crying.

When my father and mother finally got me quiet, we heard a low meowing coming from under the front porch. My father got the flashlight out of the car, and when we shined it under the porch, we saw what we already feared—Kitty Tom was lying there with froth coming out of his mouth. He was obviously suffering agonizing pain. Then we saw what had happened. Near the porch was a partially eaten squirrel. Kitty Tom had brought home one of the poisoned squirrels. He and Buster had shared it.

My father said we had to put Kitty Tom out of his misery. He went into the house and got the rifle, which I had never seen him use before, and when my back was turned, fired one shot. Then it was quiet, except for my crying.

I lay awake all night trying to imagine what my life would be like without Buster and Kitty Tom. When morning came, my father and I wrapped Buster and Kitty Tom in gunnysacks and carried them to a place in the woods near the levee. We dug two small graves side by side. After we had buried them, my father said a prayer: "Dear Lord, thank you for giving us Buster and Kitty Tom. For us, there will never be another dog and cat like them."

Later that day, I made two crosses and placed them at the head of each little grave.

THE BADGER

It's getting on toward quitting time, but the two highway maintenance men still have time to kill. They are driving slowly back to the yard in their orange truck down a black strip of Highway 395, snaking through the Mojave between the High Sierra and the Panamint Mountains.

They have been out all day, patching potholes. It is four in the afternoon, and they aren't due back until five. It is hot. They ride with the windows down and stripped to the waist. Carl is driving, and as he drives, he smokes a cigarette, flicking ashes out the window. His partner, Benny, sits with his elbow out the window, picking his nose.

Benny snags a healthy booger and tries to flick it out the window. But it's a clinger. He snaps his wrist in the wind, but the booger won't let go. Benny gives up and rolls the booger into a ball between his thumb and finger; then, aiming out into the desert, he flips it away.

"Hey, Carl," Benny says. "Pull over. I think I saw something back there."

Carl hits the brakes and pulls to the shoulder. A cloud of dust moves on down the blacktop.

"There ain't nothing out there but sagebrush," Carl says.

"No, Carl, no shit. I saw an animal. Back up, maybe it's still there."

Carl shifts to reverse, and as the truck backs up, Benny scans the desert.

"Stop! There it is!" Benny yells.

"Where?" asks Carl, leaning over for a better look.

"Right out there, about as far as you can throw a rock."

"Oh, yeah," says Carl, "now I see it. It's pretty big, ain't it? Wait a minute, Benny, I know what that is—it's a badger."

"Come on, Carl, let's see how close we can get before it runs off."

"OK," says Carl, "we got plenty of time."

The two men climb from the truck. Benny grabs his shovel; Carl looks at Benny. Then Carl grabs his shovel too, and Benny says, "Just in case."

Carl and Benny move out across the desert toward the badger. The badger watches. They walk with their shovels on their shoulders. The badger slowly shifts his weight from side to side. Halfway to the badger, they stop.

"Carl, how come he ain't running?"

"I don't know, Benny. Maybe he's curious too."

They walk on. The badger holds its ground. The closer they get, the slower they walk, as if they feared to get there. But they do. And the three of them stand there, 10 feet apart, looking at each other.

Benny points his shovel at the badger. The badger backs off. Holding his shovel like a lance, Benny moves one step toward the badger.

Suddenly, the badger stands on his hind legs. Standing, he is three feet tall. The badger bares his teeth and hisses and holds his sharp-clawed forepaws out in front like a boxer.

"Hey, Carl, look at that," Benny says, looking over his shoulder. "This sucker wants to fight."

Benny takes the shovel in both hands. "OK, Mr. badger, if it's a fight you want, you got it." And he swings the shovel at the badger. The badger jumps back and takes a swipe at the shovel with one of his front paws.

"Where are you, Carl?" asks Benny. "I may need your help."

Benny swings the shovel again. The flat of the shovel hits the badger on the shoulder, knocking him off balance. But the badger quickly recovers, hisses, and claws the air. Benny swings the shovel again. This time the edge of the shovel hits the badger in the belly. The badger goes down, but as he scrambles to get up, Carl leaps forward and swings his shovel in an overhead arc, hitting the badger in the head. One hind paw scratches the desert sand. Carl swings again. The badger lies quiet.

Standing with their hands on their shovels, Carl and Benny look down at the dead badger. Finally, Carl says, "Let's go, Benny. We gotta get back."

They shoulder their shovels and head back toward the truck. They walk like they can't wait to get out of there.

They get back in the truck, and Carl lights a cigarette. Benny leans back in his seat and says, "Carl, why did we do that?"

"I don't know, Benny."

"You know something, Carl?"

"What, Benny?"

"That was one brave badger."

Carl starts the truck, puts it in gear, and sends gravel flying getting back on the blacktop. They have to hurry now, or they'll be late getting back to the yard.

CYLINDER HEAD JOE

Cylinder Head Joe had no hair anywhere on his body. No eyebrows, no lashes, no hairs in his nose. His beardless face was smooth, almost baby-smooth—ageless. He said it was genetic on his father's side.

Cylinder Head Joe was a merchant seaman who had spent his life shipping out as a fireman. I was his shipmate on the China Bear. It was Cylinder Head Joe's last voyage. He said he was going to hang it up, "getting too old to cut the mustard," but you wouldn't know it by looking.

Cylinder Head Joe had an unusual hobby. He collected and saved small locks of pussy hair from all the women he had been with. He stored the locks of hair in little matchboxes. Each box was labeled with the woman's name, the port, and the date the lock was taken.

He kept his collection in a suitcase, a small leather suitcase of excellent quality. Only matchboxes were kept in the suitcase. Cylinder Head carried his personal gear in a seaman's canvas duffel bag.

If he liked you, and you were interested, Cylinder Head would show you his collection. For him, each box was a small capsule of time. He would pick out a box and open it, show you the lock of hair, then tell you the story about the woman it came from. He would tell you the port and the ship he was on, and tell you by name who his shipmates were. A tour through Cylinder Head Joe's collection was a tour through time and the waterfronts of the world.

I asked him once, if he had a favorite lock. He pulled a box from a special compartment, the kind that suitcases have, and said, "Yes, this one." He opened the box and showed me the lock. The hair was red, and it almost filled the box. "This is Françoise," he said. "She was from Marseilles." He lovingly fingered the lock of hair. "She was the best. I almost married her," he said. "She loved my hairless body; it drove her crazy. I never had one like her before or since."

He took a box from another compartment and showed me a lock of silky blonde hair. "This one," he said, "was the very first one. We were in high school. She thought my baldhead was cute. When we broke up, that's when I went to sea. Never saw her again, but I heard she married a barber. Can you believe that?"

During our voyage on the China Bear, Cylinder Head showed me his entire collection, lock by lock, story by story, from the South Sea Islands to Barcelona, from Montevideo to Vladivostok.

I asked Cylinder Head what would happen to his collection when he was gone. He said it was all arranged. All his locks would go with him to the crematorium. They'd all go up in flames together, and the ashes would be scattered at sea.

Some men have a passion for collecting stamps, some for collecting coins or works of art. Cylinder Head Joe had a passion for collecting locks of pussy hair and memories in a matchbox.

MARY

Her name was Mary, and she was beautiful, and she worked in the Hollywood Bar on Texas Street in Pusan, Korea.

It was early afternoon, and I sat at a table against the wall, sipping the house whiskey and chasing it with beer. I watched the whores in their miniskirts and high-heeled shoes playing cards or milling around the big, black coal-burning stove standing pot-bellied in the center of the room. On its stovetop, a dented teapot sat warming.

I watched a long pair of legs circle the stove. Then she stood at my table, hand on hip. She asked me if I liked company, and I looked up into her moonbeam face smiling down at me and said, "Sure I do."

She sat down next to me, and I asked her what she drank, and she said, "One of those," pointing at my whiskey glass. "Only I want mine with Coke."

We drank our drinks, and she told me her name–Mary; and I told her mine and she said, "I can guess the ship you on."

I said, "OK, Mary, tell me the ship I'm on."

"You on China Bear," she said. "Just get in." She pointed to a blackboard on the wall, listing the arrival and departure times of all the ships in port. "See," she said, "China Bear dock this morning, 8 o'clock."

"Oh," I said, "and I thought you were psychic."

"Why you say I'm psycho? I'm no psycho!"

"No, not psycho, psychic—like you know things."

"Yes, I know things. You better believe it," she said. And we laughed and drank more whiskey.

The jukebox played "Yellow Submarine." Mary pulled me to my feet, and we danced. My dancing was bad, but the feel of her body against mine as I held her close made me feel like Fred Astaire in heat.

As Mary rubbed her body against mine, she whispered in my ear, "We go now, yes?"

And I was ready. "Yes, let's go," I said. I bought a bottle of house whiskey and Mary got her coat.

The Hollywood Bar was one flight of steps below the street, and as we climbed the stairs, Johnny Cash was singing "A Boy Named Sue."

A chilly wind was sweeping Texas Street. I buttoned up my coat, and arm-in-arm we walked to Mary's tiny apartment: one small room with a lean-to toilet and shower. The room was cold, but Mary smiled and said, "Don't worry, soon we make it plenty warm." She then switched on a small electric heater.

I opened the bottle of booze and said, "Get some glasses, Mary, let's have a drink." She brought the glasses, and I poured the drinks. We stood by the heater, our coats still on, sipping our drinks and trying to get warm.

Then Mary downed her drink and said, "Come on, better we get warm now under covers." She turned down the blankets on the bed and said, "Come now, you get under covers. You get bed nice and warm. I be right back."

Mary took off her coat and disappeared behind the door of the lean-to toilet. I quickly stripped off all my clothes, put our drinks on a table near the bed, then leaped between the pile of icy blankets. The sheets were clean and smelled of Mary's body.

I was still shivering when Mary came through the door wearing a red kimono. "Oh, it's cold!" she said as she crossed the room, picked up an envelope from the dresser, and scurried back. She removed her kimono and, with a giggling laugh, leaped into bed. She pressed her naked body against mine, and the cool feel of Mary's flesh made me hot.

She still had the envelope in her hand, and I asked her, "Mary, what the hell is that?"

"A letter I get this morning," she said. "I no read English... You read it for me?"

"Mary, can't the letter wait till later?"

"No, please, I want to know what letter say. You read we get warm. I make you happy."

I took the envelope, and when I saw the return address, the name rang a bell. The letter was from a second mate named Phil I had sailed with on the Island Queen. Now, I felt both curious and guilty—a snoop seeing things he's not meant to see.

I opened the letter and started to read: "My dearest Mary, I miss you so much. Hope you miss me as much as I miss you. My ship should be in Pusan by the first of March. But I don't have to tell you that, do I? You know my schedule as well as I do."

Mary laid a now warm leg over mine and rested her head on my chest, as though she were listening to the beat of my heart.

In a state of growing arousal, I read on: "Mary, have you been giving any thought to all the things we talked about last time I was there? I have thought of little else. The big problem, as you know, is my wife. She says she will never give me a divorce. Thank the Lord we never had any kids but would love to have one or two with you."

Mary had slipped her hand around my cock, and as I read, she caressed it gently. I started to lay the letter aside, but Mary said, "No, finish letter, please."

So, I read on with divided interest: "Somehow, Mary, I'll bring you to the States. Divorce or no divorce, I'll find a way. Meantime, Mary darling, we must cherish the few short hours that we can spend together."

Raising her head from my chest, Mary asked, "What means cherish?"

And I thought for a while and said, "To hold something close to the heart."

"Oh," Mary said, laying her head back down and continuing to fondle my cock.

I continued on, reading rapidly: "You are the best woman I ever had, and Mary, it's true, I can't be happy until I can have you all to myself. I am mailing this from San Francisco. The ship sails tonight at 0100, so I will be in Pusan very soon. Be patient, Mary. We will work it out. Trust me. You will be my one and only. Must get this in the mail. All my love, Phil."

I dropped the one-page letter to the floor and ran my fingers through Mary's long black hair. She raised her head, and I pulled her to me. We kissed as Mary climbed on top of me. She slowly lowered herself, taking me up inside of her with a low, gasping moan.

That evening, I learned why Phil was so in love. Mary knew the tricks to make men happy. She knew how to keep them coming back for more.

We made love, we drank, we made love and drank some more. I fell asleep, then awoke with a start. I looked at my watch. It was almost 12. I had to hurry; I had the midnight watch.

I threw back the covers and jumped out of bed. Mary said, "What's the matter? Where you go?"

"Back to the ship," I said, "to go on watch."

Mary got up and put on her kimono. "I go toilet," she said. "I be right back." I got dressed quickly, and before she returned, I left her some money on the dresser.

I was at the door when Mary returned. "One minute," she said, "I give you something." She went to the dresser, glanced at the money, and took a slip of paper from a box. She pressed the slip of paper in my hand, and as I kissed her on the cheek, she said, "This my address. You write me letter, yes?"

I kissed her on the other cheek and said, "I'm not good at writing letters, Mary."

I said goodbye and stepped out into the cold. From the doorway, Mary called out, "Tony!" This was the first time she had used my name. I thought perhaps she had forgotten it. "Don't forget to write me letter, Tony."

I turned and waved and said, "Goodnight, Mary."

The wind was cold. I turned up my collar and headed for Texas Street to hail a cab. It was late, and I had the midnight watch.

AFTERWARD

Yes, it's true! Initially, freelance editor Ramya Srinivasan and I thought we'd produce two books of Glen's written works. When Ramya moved on in her life and away from the Bay Area, I was on my own to decide what to do. So I thought book one would contain just the best of Glen's poetry Ramya and I had selected, but that would have made the book less than 100 pages.

Then, I had the extreme good fortune to speak with Nancy Schulman, a longtime friend of Glen and me. She said the book would be way too short, and since Nancy loves to read, I listened to her advice. She said, why not include more of his writings in book one. After just a minute of thought, I said, "Yes, that's it!" But Nancy didn't hesitate and added, "What about his art?" She knew what a remarkable, self-taught artist he was. I told her that book two would feature his art and would have information about his evolution as an artist.

Nancy and I were both excited, and now I had to find others who would produce Glen's book since Ramya was no longer available. As it turns out, I was in luck. Bill Knowland, owner and producer of Direct Images Interactive, and Donna Tate, a web developer, had worked with me before. I have known both of them since 2014, and they were on board immediately. They were joined by Janice Lalley, an editor and proofreader. Together, they have made this project such an overwhelmingly pleasant and wonderful experience.

In addition to poetry, we added Glen's flash fiction stories, which are really special and cover wide-ranging subjects: condensed but guaranteed to remain a long time in the mind of a reader.

And finally, there are Glen's short stories. Ramya and I had selected many excellent short stories, but I knew using them all in this book would make it way too long. I didn't hesitate in selecting the five stories that appear here. They are a great sampling of Glen's own sense of his history, his humor, and his humanity and are beautifully written.

—Ellen Sarkisian Chesnut

OTHER WORKS BY THE AUTHOR

Taking the Bull by the Horns

Of Time and the Leaky Faucet

ABOUT THE AUTHOR

"A little about myself. I was born in Amarillo, Texas. I graduated from California State University at Fresno and served a two-year hitch in the army. After the army, I've made my living as a merchant seaman. My artwork has been exhibited in Northern California galleries and museums.

My poetry and prose have appeared in various magazines and journals, including, ZYZZYVA, PEARL, CHICAGO QUARTERLY REVIEW, UNDER THE RADAR, THE SOUTH DAKOTA REVIEW, THE 33 REVIEW, OVER THE TRANSOM, MAIN STREET RAG. I have two books: TAKING THE BULL BY THE HORNS by the 3300 Press, and OF TIME AND THE LEAKY FAUCET by the ex Nihilo Press."—Glen Chesnut

This statement appeared in all of the submissions Glen sent out, whether they were poetry or short stories.

One of the editors of NERVE COWBOY, Joseph Shields, held a special place in Glen's heart as Joseph always included a note when something was accepted (many times) or rejected.

In his life span of 87 years, Glen's younger years covered an America long gone. In his youth, a boy could take a leave of absence from high school and work as a cowboy, which he did. Shipping out as a merchant seaman, which he did for over 20 years, always held the promise of adventures for Glen in the Ports of Call. The ships he boarded would dock for at least a couple of days in each place, giving him the chance to see the sights and meet people. Today, the turnaround time for a container ship in port is often a little more than 24 hours.

He never forgot where he came from, and that's why I am including information about his parents. He was the youngest son of six siblings: four boys and two girls. His father, Sam, was one of the last of the cowboys who punched cattle on the open range in Texas and in the badlands of Wyoming. Sam was born on April 11, 1899, 60 miles from Amarillo, Texas. At the age of 13, he was a full ranch hand with a string of six cow ponies assigned to him.

On February 25, 1917, at the age of 17, Sam was married to his 19-year-old childhood sweetheart, Ulta Hopkins, whom he met during a brief stay in the Ozarks of Missouri in 1912. Ulta, better known as Chessie, cooked at the ranch where Sam worked as a bronco buster and cowhand. She was well known for her sourdough biscuits that the cowboys called "high top biscuits."

Of those early years, Sam said, "I broke a lot of wild horses. In those days, the cow horse was out of mustang mares. Most of them were mean to the day they died. We didn't know how to train horses the way they do now. Oh, we would train them to be good cow horses, but they were not gentle."

Sam and Chessie were baptized in the Reorganized Church of the Latter-Day Saints, and Sam was ordained a priest in 1937. When they lived in central California, he ministered to the sick, buried the dead, and baptized and preached the gospel. In all ways, Chessie was his faithful helper.

In his later years, Sam worked as a cattle foreman for the Crofton ranch, running about 10,000 herds of cattle, and as manager and partner of the Wrigley ranch.

Always a lover of horses, Sam owned a beautiful stallion named Ace that took first place in every show he was entered. Among cowmen, Sam was a legend as a cowman and minister.

Sam, however, could not stay in one place too long, and his son, Glen, remembered that the family moved 12 times before he completed high school. That's just the way it was with his father. No hard feelings on Glen's part, another day and another adventure.

In 1966, Glen visited New Orleans and struck up a friendship with Roman Rome, the owner of THE PAPERBACK BOOK STORE on South Rampart Street. They corresponded for a year after Glen went back to San Francisco. Roman encouraged Glen to continue writing and to submit his paintings to galleries, which he did years later.

When I first met Glen in 1970, he used a room in his apartment on Julian Avenue in the Mission District of San Francisco as an artist studio. There were canvasses stacked up along the walls, an artist easel, and second-hand tables laden with paints and brushes.

We married in 1972, and a year later moved to Sanchez Street, where we lived for 35 eventful years. Glen transformed the unused upper floor of our Edwardian flats into an enormous artist studio. He'd sit on an old maroon upholstered chair and hold hours-long conversations with his best friend, Bob Kilduff. Often, he would just think, sketch, and read books that he bought in a bookstore on 24th Street in the Noe Valley. Glen continued creating art regularly for about 20 years, submitted pieces to galleries, and had a two-person art show with fellow artist, Karol Barske. He loved what he was doing.

I don't recall when he lost his desire to go up to his attic studio and create large-format paintings. He was writing again. It just so happened at that time that he bought a brand new Mac computer and set up a tiny office in the alcove underneath the foot of the stairs to his attic studio. Glen taught himself how to use the Mac and began writing regularly. Then as luck would have it, he discovered the poetry readings at the 3300 Club on Mission Street in San Francisco. He met a fellow writer and poet, Jonathan Hayes, and a friendship blossomed.

He wrote every day and started sending out his writings to small publishing houses and journals. His work was recognized as original and began to be published much to his satisfaction. Glen did create art, but smaller, multi-media works often incorporating his words. His writings were also published in the periodical, OVER THE TRANSOM, which was edited by Jonathan Hayes. His hilarious cartoons appeared in the journal. Really special, however, were the covers: copies of photographs taken by Glen while a private in the army and stationed in Germany in the 1950s. He was delighted by the positive reviews of his work.

In 2006, Glen and I moved to Alameda from our place in San Francisco. It was a big adjustment for him as he loved the city and our home there.

But Glen continued writing and submitting poetry and short stories to various periodicals and journals. At the same time, he was affiliated with the Frank Bette Center for the Arts. All of the pieces he submitted were accepted, and he even won a best in show for his painting, THE CHEF.

What fun I had being married to Glen for 45 years. SOME-TIMES FIREWORKS CAN LAST A LIFETIME.

—Ellen Sarkisian Chesnut

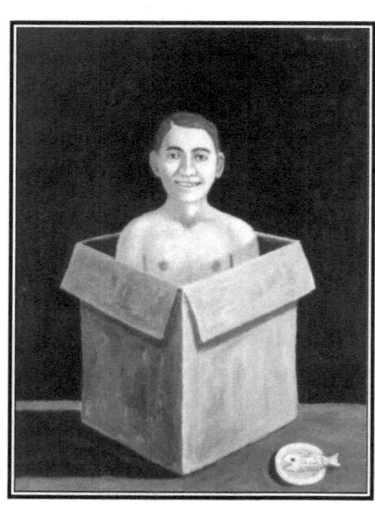